Sidney Smith Rider

## Supplement to the Rhode Island Colonial Records

Comprising a List of the Freemen Admitted from May, 1747, to May, 1754

Sidney Smith Rider

**Supplement to the Rhode Island Colonial Records**
*Comprising a List of the Freemen Admitted from May, 1747, to May, 1754*

ISBN/EAN: 9783337160920

Printed in Europe, USA, Canada, Australia, Japan

Cover: Foto ©Andreas Hilbeck / pixelio.de

More available books at **www.hansebooks.com**

# RHODE ISLAND COLONIAL RECORDS

COMPRISING

## A LIST OF THE FREEMEN ADMITTED

FROM

MAY, 1747, TO MAY, 1754.

PROVIDENCE:

SIDNEY S. RIDER.

1875·

RHODE ISLAND (Colony)  Records... 1856-65.
   (Supplement card)

— —— Supplement to the Rhode Island colonial
records, comprising a list of the freemen admitted from May, 1747, to May, 1754.    Providence,Rider,1875.

   48p.

—— —— another copy of the supplement.

## LIST OF. FREEMEN. ADMITTED. TO THE COLONY.

### TUESDAY, MAY. 5th,. 1747.

The persons whose names here follow, having taken the oath or affirmation prescribed by the law of this colony against bribery and corruption, are hereby admitted to give their votes to choose officers for their respective towns, and also to give their votes for the choice of the general officers in the colony :—

### NEWPORT.

Peleg Brown, Walter Chaloner, Hezekiah Carpenter, Samuel Wickham, John Channing, Robert Carr, Walter Cranston, Nathaniel Potter, Daniel Updike, Peter Bours, Godfrey Mallbone, James Honeyman, Jun'r., William Read, Thomas Freebody, Mathew Robinson, Lodowick Updike, Job Bennet, Jun'r., William Dyre, Jun'r., Daniel Dunham, Thomas Cranston, Gideon Wanton, Samuel Rodman, John Easton, Serg't. Daniel Goddard, Stephen Tripp, James Sheffield, Henry Taggart, Job Bennet, John Tillinghast, Thomas Wickham, Samuel Freebody, George Wanton, Philip Wilkinson, Jonathan Tillinghast, Benjamin Hall, William Benson, Caleb Peckham, Joseph Wanton, Elisha Johnson, John Cranston, Thomas Richardson, Clarke Rodman, Benjamin Haszard, Nicholas Easton, Jonathan Easton, Samuel Collins, Abraham Redwood, Charles Whitefield, Stephen Wanton, Peter Easton, Peleg Wood,

Jun'r., James Wanton, Gideon Wanton, Jun'r., Caleb Carr, John
Shearman, John Easton, Philip Wanton, Samuel Dyre, Robert
Taylor, John Gardner, Nicholas Carr, Joseph Whipple, Samuel
Carr, Jonathan Bowers, Abraham Coggeshall, Peleg Thurston,
James Coggeshall, Gideon Cornel, Abraham Borden, Benjamin
Borden, Jonathan Marsh, Peter Thurston, Mathew Pates, Timothy
Waterhouse, Thomas Rodman, son of Samuel, Elisha Coggeshall,
Benjamin Thurston, Joseph Freeborn, Jacob Barney, Samuel
Holmes, Benjamin Tayre, John Tayre, John Bennet, Benjamin
Stanton, Jun'r., Elisha Sandford, Josiah Coggeshall, Samuel
Thurston, Jun'r., Caleb Earl, Joseph Slocum, Joseph Scott, James
Gould, William Corey, John Freebody, Jun'r., John Rogers, Si-
mon Rhodes, John Baley, Nathan Carpenter, John Stephens, Rouse
Potter, John Dawley, Benjamin Jefferson, Nehemiah Marks, Rich-
ard Roes, Richard Clark, Robert Stevens, Benjamin Wyatt, John
Rogers, son of Peleg, Jeremiah Child, Jeremiah Child, Jun'r.,
Thomas Melvil, Benjamin Pitman, Jacob Dehane, Samuel Pitman,
Isaac Stelle, Peter Bowdin, Martin Howard, Daniel Ayrault, Jun'r.,
Benjamin Willson, Herbert Nichols, Joseph Baley, Evan Mallbone,
Fones Haszard, John Beard, Jonathan Nichols, Ebenezer Richardson,
Jonathan Thurston, Daniel Shrieve, William Ellery, Timothy
Peckham, Christopher Lyndsey, Daniel Smith, Ezekiel Burroughs,
John Sawdy, Henry Sabin, Benoni Gardner, Edward Boss, John
Fryers, Thomas Coggeshall, Thomas Chadwick, John Dennis,
cooper, Joshua Sawyer, Samuel Ward, John Bennet, mariner, Si-
mon Pease, Caleb Gardner, Job Townsend, Constant Baley, Na-
thaniel Norton, Robert Shearman, John Goddard, son of Daniel,
Nathaniel Coggeshall, Samuel Lyndon, Jun'r., Joseph Whipple,
Jun'r., Peter Coggeshall, James Carey, John Peckham, Joseph
Ireson, George Gibbs, Joseph Warren, George Wanton, Jun'r., Rob-
ert Bridges, Jonathan Nichols, innholder, Richard Wilson, Thomas
Rogers, John Peirce, James Tew, Grindal Thurston, David Seaver, Is-
rael Chapman, Peleg Barker, John Gibbs, James Allen, Nathaniel
Langley, Isaac Ingraham, John Simpson, John Simpson, Jun'r.,
William Clagget, Robert Kelly, William Woodward, Oliver Beere,
William Burroughs, Benjamin Norton, James Lyon, Wing Spooner,
Joshua Lyon, Joseph Atwood, Samuel Crandal, William Grafton,
Isaac Bowen, Isaac Bowen, Jun'r., James Sisson, James Nichols,
Elisha Shearman, John Ingraham, Peter Cossens, Joseph Sand-
ford, Benjamin Sherburn, Philip Tillinghast, John Archer John

Doublin, Nathaniel Grafton, John Chapman, Samuel Lyndon, Robert Sisson, John Tanner, Joseph Weeden, Peter Buliod, Sion Arnold, William Higgins, John Brown, distiller, John Belitho, John Brown, merchant, Edward Lillibridge, James Tanner, Joseph Sylvester, William Wyatt, John Brown, Jun'r., (son of John Brown, merchant,) Edward Scott, Oliver White, Alexander Swan, William Almy, James Milward, William Tate, Gendefer Lyndey, Benjamin Nichols, son of Jonathan Nichols, innholder, Daniel Vaughan, Samuel Weeden, Thomas Jeffries, Benjamin Jeffries, son of Thomas, Edward Boss, Jun'r., George Goulding, Zepheniah Pease, William Sanford, John Wharkman, George Thomas, William Heffernan, William Heffernan, Jun'r., John Pitman, Robert Carter, Daniel Dunham, Jun'r., John Jeffries, miller, John Pitman, son of Benjamin, James Fitz Gerald, Simon Newton, Jonathan Heath, Rufus Church, Samuel Burroughs, Joseph Sabin, Miller Frost, James Burgis, Joseph Tillinghast, Jun'r., Benjamin Carr, Benjamin Holt, Job Caswell, William Coddington, William Coddington, Jun'r., Kendal Nichols, Joseph Sanford, Jr., son of Joseph Sanford, John Mundon, Samuel Phillips, Jonathan Crandal, Josias Lyndon, William Brenton, Kendal Nichols, Jun'r., Henry Bliss, George Haszard, Samuel Haszard, Benjamin Nichols, John Tweedy, Pardon Tillinghast, Jeremiah Clark, Thomas Ward, John Baley.

- PROVIDENCE.

Stephen Hopkins, Richard Waterman, Jun'r., John Aplin, George Taylor, Jeremiah Field, Amaziah Waterman, Obediah Brown, Jun'r., William Ashton, Zuriel Waterman, John Whipple, Jun'r., John Angel, Ephraim Bowen, George Brown, Daniel Smith, Joseph Harris, Thomas Harris, Alexander Frazier, Thomas Harding, Joseph Wanton, James Brown, John Potter, James Mitchel, William Fenner, Benjamin Potter, Jun'r., Edward Trip, Samuel Chace, John Andrew, Edward Sheldon, William Pearce, Silas Field, Jeremiah Smith, Isaac White, Thomas Harris, Jun'r., Thomas Fenner, Jun'r., Nathan Angel, John Waterman, Jun'r., Joseph Waterman, Nathaniel Day, Joseph Borden, Jun'r., Joseph Potter, Fearnot Packard, Daniel Fenner, Joseph Shelldon, William Stone, Thomas Olney, Jun'r., Philip Sheldon, Joseph Olney, Peter Burlingame, Edward Kinnicut, Christopher Harris, William Westcot, Daniel Sprague, Moses

Burlingame, Jun'r., Henry Paget, Samuel Ladd, John Wanton, William Rhodes, Joseph Fenner, Henry Harris, John Olney, Samuel Currie, Simon Smith, Christopher Waterman, Jonathan Hammon, Peleg Williams, Jun'r., Amos Westcot, Charles Olney, Josias Thornton, Benjamin Hunt, Allin Brown, Samuel Boyles, John Angel, Jun'r., Daniel Mathewson, Elisha Green, Edward Fenner, Edward Thurber, John Dexter, Jun'r., Jabez Bowen, Joseph Field, Stephen Remington, Benjamin Cushing, Benjamin Whipple, Abraham Shedon, Israel Gibbs, Joseph Angel, Uriah Hernden, Nathaniel Williams, Isaiah Hawkins, Jonathan Randal, Joseph Olney, Jun'r., Thomas Whipple, Jun'r., Samuel Westcot, Thomas Fenner, the 3d, Jonathan Stone, Elisha Tillinghast, Jabez Westcot, Neriah Waterman, Benjamin Gorham, Johua Remington, Joseph Brown, William Hopkins, Jonathan Olney, Richard Waterman, the 3d, Elisha Brown, Robert Gibbs, Richard Fenner, Daniel Abbot, William Rhodes, Jun'r., John Dexter, Richard Matthewson, Philip Tillinghast, Gideon Crawford, Daniel Jenckes, Elijah Dean, John Mason, Christopher Arnold, Benjamin Belknap, Joseph Remington, Thomas Edmonds, Benoni Potter, James Greene, Benjamin Westcot, son of Stukely, Richard Brown, Jun'r., Phineas Brown, Joseph Fisk, Samuel Aborn, Elezer Westcot, Hope Corpe, John Birkit, Sukely Westcot, Joshua Ashton, Robert Knight, Peter Newcom, Joseph Thornton, Israel Mathewson, Thomas Field, Jun'r., John Brown, Jun'r., John Burton. Jun'r., Christopher Lippit, Joseph Coman, Jeremiah Jenckes, John Hoyle, Jun'r., Mathew Manchester, Jereiah Hawking, Samuel Dyre, David Harris, William Tillinghast, Archibald Young, John Randal, Ebenezer Bats, John Gorton, Henry Randal, John Corpe, Zechariah Matthewson, Ezekiel Warner, William Randal, William Brown, Jr., William Brown, Joseph Randal, Robert Sterry, Thomas Fenner, Joseph Williams, Jun'r., Jonathan Knight, Jun'r., Roger Burlingame, John Stone, Daniel Dye, Joseph Williams, son of James, John Whipple, Thomas Williams, Joseph Randal, caulker, Peter Sprague, Richard Fenner, Jun'r., Peter Tift, John Warner, Peter Tift, Jun'r., John Potter Jun'r., John Mawney, Christo: Burlingame, James Hoyle, Timothy Carpenter, William Basson, John Cumstock, Thomas Olney, Joseph Snow, Thomas Kinnicut, Obediah Brown, Richard Thornton, Jun'r., Elisha Baker, John Clarke, John Pain, Jeremiah Merethow, Ebenezer Jenckes, Samuel Cumstock, Robert Knight, Jun'r., John Batte, William Roberts, Joseph Jenckes, William Holden, William Hammon, Jun'r.

## PORTSMOUTH.

John Shearman, Jun'r., Josiah Lawton, Stephen Brownel, Esq'r.,
Robert Lawton, Esq'r., William Sandford, Gideon Freeborn, Esq'r.,
Joseph Dennis, Esq'r., William Anthony, Jun'r., Esq'r., Benjamin
Tucker, Esq'r., Jonathan Freeborn, Gideon Durfie, Esq'r., Joseph
Martin, Thomas Hicks, Esq'r., Benjamin Hicks, Esq'r., Benjamin
Fish, Caleb Bennet, Benjamin Freeborn, George Cornel, Esq'r.,
Daniel Howland, Esq'r., William Hall, Esq'r., Peleg Shearman,
Stephen Brayton, Esq'r., Gideon Anthony, David Lake, William
Brightman, Joseph Martin, Jun'r., Col. Jeremiah Lawton, Walter
Cornel, Esq'r., William Anthony, Esq'r., George Thomas, Gideon
Freeborn, Jun'r., David Anthony, Capt. Job Lawton, Giles Slocum,
Jr., Esq'r., Benjamin Shearman, John Shrieve, Peleg Shearman,
Jun'r., Francis Brayton, Daniel Howland, Jun'r., William Cornel,
Esq'r., Thomas Shearman, Esq'r., Mathew Slocum, Oliver Earl,
Thomas Tripp, Capt. William Arnold, Edward Perry, Richard Cor-
nel, John Shrieve, Jun'r., George Lanson, John Shearman, Jun'r.,
Caleb Hill, Esq'r., Preserved Shearman, Jonathan Pearce, William
Earl, Esq'r., Joseph Thomas, Joseph Anthony, Anthony Cory,
Thomas Manchester, John Shearman, Thomas Brownel, John
Butts, Silas Tallman, Benjamin Tallman, Jun'r., John Sisson, John
Sisson, Jun'r.

## WARWICK.

William Greene, Esq'r., James Arnold, Esq'r., Philip Greene,
Esq'r., Jeremiah Lippit, Esq'r., Capt. William Arnold, Mr. Fones
Greene, Maj. Peter Greene, Capt. William Arnold, son of William,
Mr. David Greene, Col. Randal Holdon, John Greene, Esq., Mr.
Francis Matteson, Col. Benoni Waterman, John Holdon, son of
Charles, Mr. Moses Lippit, Capt. Charles Holdon, Mr. Daniel
Greene, Capt. Elisha Greene, Capt. James Green, Jabez Greene,
Esq'r., Mr. Malachi Rhodes, Mr. Barlo Greene, Mr. Elisha Arnold,
Jun'r., Mr. Richard Greene, Jr., Richard Greene, Esq'r., Mr. Rob-
ert Wickes, Mr. John Wells, Joseph Stafford, Esq'r., Philip Arnold,
Esq., Mr. Joseph Lippit, Benjamin Greene, Jos'h. Edmunds, John
Rice. John Walton, William Greene, son of William, John Rhodes,
Anthony Low, Samuel Stafford, James Green, son of William,
Benjamin Earle, Elisha Arnold, Christopher Smith, Cotten Palmer,

William Arnold, son of Elisha, Josiah Arnold, Samuel Gorton, Benja. Pearce, Charles Rhodes, Thomas Remington, John Corpe, Jun'r., John Warner, Josiah Arnold, Jun'r., John Greene, son of Peter, Randal Rice, Joseph Edmonds, Jun'r., Abraham Chace, Adam Casey, Thomas Rice, Samuel Barton, Edward Case, Stephen Low, James Rhoades, Benjamin Greene, son of William, John Rhoades, Jun'r., James Arnold, Jr., Jonathan Greene, John Low, Jun'r., Elisha Baker, Oliver Carpenter, Thomas Fry, John Warner, Jun'r., John Stone, Othniel Gorton, Elisha Brown, Silas Baker, Thankful Collins, Robert Westgate, Henry Rice, Thomas Wickes, son of John, dec'd., Eliezer Whipple, Josiah Arnold, son of Josiah, John Holdon, Rufus Barton, Jr., Ebenezer Slocum, William Warner, Moses Badlong, Resolved Waterman, James Carder, Caleb Arnold, Simon Arnold, Benjamin Ellis, Amos Lockwood, Stephen Colegrove, John Carder, Jun'r., Philip Baker, Andrew Barton, John Levalley, Edward Casey, Aaron Davis, Benjamin Tallman, Thomas Camstock, Philip Sweet, Jun'r., John Battey, Peter Cammet, John Matteson, John Greene, James Greene, Increase Green, William Battey, Benjamin Arnold, Richard Estes, Anthony Barton, Samuel Greene, John Holdon, Jun'r., John Carder, Adam Lockwood, George Wightman, Jun'r., Edward Gorton, Benoni Price, Jeremiah Randal, Thom's. Arnold, Mathew Sweet, Nathan Westcot, William Tibbits, John Wightman, Thomas Rice, Jun'r., Henry Matteson, Peter Levalley.

### WESTERLY.

George Babcock, William Babcock, Oliver Babcock, Joseph Pendleton, Silas Greenman, William Hern, Benjamin Randal, Joseph Champlin, Edward Saunders, Nathaniel Lewis, Hubb'd Burdick, Thomas Clark, Joshua Clark, Thomas Hiscox, Jeremiah Angel, Stephen Babcock, Richard Berry, Daniel Mackoon, John Maxson, Benjamin Chase, John Lewis, Nathan Tanner, Ichabod Babcock, Joshua Thompson, Joseph Pendleton, Jun'r., Thomas Potter, Josias Hill, Matthew Greene, Gideon Worden, Benjamin Hall, Jun'r., Thomas Edwards, Nathan Burdick, George Stillman, Thomas Wells, Jun'r., Stephen Lewis, John Crandal, (son to Peter,) John Lewis, the 3d, Edward Bleaven, William Hiscox, Joseph Crandal, Peter Crandal, William Pendleton, Samuel Babcock, Francis West, Joshua Babcock, Eber Crandal, Nathan Babcock, William Champ-

lin, William Ross, Simon Ray, Edmund Pendleton, Jun'r., Benoni
Smith, Ebenezer Rathbun, Jeremiah Clark, William Davis, John
Cottril, Jun'r., Samuel Hill, George Thurston, Ezekiel Gavit, Jo-
seph Lawton, Samuel Gavit, John Saunders, Joseph Lewis, Jun'r.
James Wells, Joseph Crandal, Jun'r., Judiah Irish, Isaac Sheffield,
Richard Deake, John Lewis, (son of Esq'r. John,) John Halls,
Elisha Lewis, Joshua Vose, William Davis, (son to Peter) Samuel
Saunders, Joseph Saunders, Hezekiah Collins, Jonathan Lewis,
Stephen Saunders, John Hall, Jun'r., David Willcox, John Larkin.

### NEW SHOREHAM.

Capt. Edward Sands, Capt. Robert Hull, Samuel Rath'un,
Jun'r., Nathaniel Littlefield, John Mott, William Dodge, Samuel
Rathbun, Thomas Dickens, Daniel Rose, Caleb Littlefield, John
Littlefield, Thomas Pain, Samuel Dodge, John Pain, Abel Frank-
lin Jun'r., Nathaniel Mott, Jonathan Mitchel, Thomas Mitchel,
John Dodge, Henry Gardner, Stephen Frankling, Joseph Mitchel,
Jun'r.

### NORTH KINGSTOWN.

George Tibbits, Thomas Hill, Beriah Brown, Robert Eldred,
Samuel Dyre, Caleb Clarke, Ebenezer Brown, Alexander Brown,
George Thomas, Daniel Coggeshall, Samuel Thomas, Benoni Sweet,
Immanuel Northup, Thomas Phillips, Robert Brownel, James
Sweet, Thomas Allen, John Cole, (son of Elisha,) Edward Cole,
Jacob Finder, Nicholas Northup. Ephraim Gardner, Jeremiah
Gardner, William Tanner, James Gardner, Rowse Helme, Jun'r.
John Pinder, William Chadsey, James Cowper, Benjamin Allen,
Elisha Clarke, Jeffry Davis, Peter Tourge, Thomas Allen, Jun'r.,
Edward Dyre, Jun'r., Robert Northup, Ezekiel Gardner, Robert
Havens, Francis Willet, Robert Havens, Jun'r., Peter Reynolds,
Robert Haszard, William Spencer, Benjamin Congdon, Benjamin
Watson, Job Tripp, Stephen Card, James Eldred, Benjamin Cong-
don, Jun'r., Daniel Fones, James Fones, James Wightman, Daniel
Greene, Stephen Shearman, Henry Wall, Ebenezer Slocum, Thomas
Hill, Jun'r., Jeremiah Haszard, Philip Aylsworth, Thomas Tourge,
Stephen Northup, Enoch Place, Palmer Tanner, Francis Briggs,
William Tanner, Jun'r., Arthur Aylsworth, Nathaniel Berry, Jo-

2

seph Jess, William Dyre, Benjamin Greene, Joseph Case, Christopher Spencer, Christopher Hall, Thomas Lawton, John Kingsley, Samuel Browning, Jun'r., Benedict Eldred, James Boone, Ephraim Mitchel, Joseph Northup, Jun'r., Charles Brown, Jun'r., Thomas Scranton, Thomas Nichols, John Congdon, Thomas Sweet, Thomas Spencer, Eber Shearman, (son to William,) John Reynolds, Jun'r., Sawell Kingsley, Joseph Congdon, Charles Brown, Robert Westcoat, Eber Shearman, Samuel Boone, Jun'r., Abial Tripp, John Weest, Jabez Chadsey, William William Sweet.

### SOUTH KINGSTOWN.

Jeffry Watson, Esq'r., Stephen Haszard, Esq'r., Jeremiah Niles, Esq'r., Capt. Robert Haszard, Mr. William Mumford, Samuel Babcock, Esq'r., Mr. John Potter, Isaac Sheldon, Esq'r., Thomas Brown, Esq'r., Jeremiah Brown, Esq'r., Mr. William Gardner, Mr. Daniel Shearman, Doct. Robert Haszard, Thomas Haszard, (son of Robert,) Mr. Henry Gardner, Jun'r., Mr. Benjamin Barber, Capt. Job Babcock, Mr. Benjamin Peckcom, Jun'r., Mr. John Babcock, Mr. Immanuel Case, Mr. William Smith, Mr. Stephen Tift, Mr. Joseph Phillips, Mr. Rowland Robinson, Col. Elisha Reynolds, Capt. James Helme, Latham Clarke, Paul Woodbridge, James Easton, George Gardner, Nathaniel Helme, Robert Potter, John Case, Esq'r., Edmund Sheffield, Samuel Babcock, Nathaniel Niles, Mr. William Brown, Mr. William Robinson, Mr. Samuel Tift, Mr. Samuel Tift, Jun'r., Maj. Thomas Haszard, Messrs. John Gardner, William Haszard, Capt. Samuel Niles, Messrs. Robert Haszard, Jeffry Haszard, John Reynolds, John Steadman, Peleg Peckcom, John Natson, Jun'r., Thomas Hopkins, Robert Brown, Caleb Gardner, William Potter. John Browning, Sanford Case, Thomas Cottril, Caleb Westcot, Tennent Tift, Thomas Steadman, Nathan Tift, Stephen Champlin, George Gardner, Jun'r., Stephen Haszard, Jun'r., John Hookey, Joseph Hammond, Philip Shearman, Benjamin Haszard, Jonathan Otley, William Taylor, William Congdon, John Gardner, (son of William,) Samuel Brown, Benjamin Peckcom, John Potter, (Taylor,) Adam Gould, Jeremiah Browning, Paul Niles, Stephen Cottril, William Gardner, Jun'r., Thomas Gardner, Solomon Carpenter, Joseph Holway, Thomas Browning, Nathan Gardner, William Browning, and Joseph Hull.

Thomas Fry, Jun'r., Giles Peirce, John Fry, William Spencer, Christopher Vaughan, John Peirce, (s. Jeremiah,) John Spencer, s. William,) Joshua Coggeshall, Philip Tillinghast, Christopher Vaughan, Jun'r., Edmund Johnson, Thomas Spencer, Jeremiah Peirce, John Spencer, Joseph Nicholls, Benjamin Briggs, Samuel Soule, John Ollin, Nathan Ried, John Spencer, (s. of Peleg,) Alexander Nichols, William Wall, Thomas Spencer, (boatman,) Thomas Spencer, (s. Jno.) John Arnold, John Spencer, Jun'r., Thomas Cossey, Joseph Spencer, William Spencer, (s. Peleg,) Richard Briggs, Thomas Coggeshall, John Peirce. Jun'r., Richard Weaver, Thomas Pearce, Abner Spencer, (s. Michael,) Jonathan Corey, William Spencer, Jun'r., Joseph Stafford, Ebenezer Cook, John Coggeshall, Abiel Hall, Rufus Spencer, Gideon Brayton, Giles Peirce, (s. Jno., John Spencer, (son Michael,) Peter Mawney, Rufus Greene, Jonathan Weaver, Thomas Nichols, William Cass, Samuel Gardner, William Bennet, John Weaver, Daniel Peirce, Samuel Darris, Daniel Vaughan, Henry Gardner, John Gardner, schoolmaster, William Andrew, Caleb Vaughan, Caleb Bealy, Benjamin Sweet, Jun'r., George Vaughan, Ebenezer Goddard, William Card, John Underwood, Henry Sweet.

## JAMESTOWN.

Daniel Weeden, Joseph Clarke, Thomas Carr, Joseph Underwood, William Martin, John Cranston, Samuel Clarke, John Paine, Abel Franklin, John Martin, Teddeman Hull, Job Howland, William Tew, George Franklin, Samuel Slocum, Edward Carr, Jun'r.

## SMITHFIELD.

William Arnold, Esq'r., William Gulley, David Cumstock, Esq'r., John Aldrich, Esq'r., Samuel Winsor, Thomas Steere. Esq'r., Thomas Lapham, Peter Aldrich, Jonathan Arnold, John Winsor, Gideon Cumstock, John Smith, Joseph Lapham, Benjamin Lapham, Barleston Brayton, Resolved Waterman, William Jenckes, Esq'r., Joseph Mowry, (son of Capt. Daniel,) Enoch Barnes, Thomas Sayles, David Wilkinson, Doct. John Jencks, Thomas Owen, Thomas Arnold, Jun'r., Capt. Daniel Mowry, Silvanus Aldrich, Benjamin Wilkinson, James Appleberry, Joseph Smith, Jun'r., Abra'm. Winsor, Othniel Mathewson, Robert Staples.

## SCITUATE.

Messrs. Charles Harris, James Brown, Benjamin Fisk, Job Randal, John Edwards, James Calvin, Gideon Harris, Benjamin Fisk, Jun'r., Gideon Hamman, Hezekiah Fisk, Thomas Angel, Job Fisk, Christopher Smith, Jun'r., John Fisk, Thomas Ralph, Jun'r., Judah Brown, Silvanus Wight, Edward Potter, John Edwards, Jun'r., John Borden, Samuel Darrance, James Darrance, George Darrance, Jun'r., John Darrance, Jun'r., John Bates, Daniel Fisk, Jeddediah Harris, John Hallet, John Tyler, Benjamin Coman, William Tyler, Jeremiah Mathewson, and John King, Jun'r.

### GLOCESTER.

Andrew Brown, Richard Steere, Zebedee Hopkins, Isaiah Inman, Elijah Hawins, Abra'm. Tourtelot, William Coman, Richard Smith, Amaziah Harris, Abner Bartlet, Walter Phetteplace, Timothy Wilmoth, James Blackaman, Nehemiah Sprague, Hosea Steere, Abraham Tourtelot, Jun'r., William Hawkins, Stephen Smith, Jun'r., Elisha Eddy, Wait Smith, John Cowen, James Cowen, Elijah Inman, Hosanna Brown, Israel Arnold, Benjamin Smith, Ezekiel Smith, David Aldrich, James Sweet, Clement King, Ezra Bartlet, Edward Inman, and Daniel Bartlet.

### CHARLESTOWN.

Samuel Perry, Joseph Stanton, Christopher Champlin, James Congdon, John Hill, Samuel Clark, James Rogers, Benjamin James, John Hickes, Richard Baley, William Congdon, Thomas Kinyon, Jun'r., Nathaniel Potter, Joseph Hoxsie, Joseph Eanoss, John Hill, Jun'r., Joseph Eanoss, Jun'r., John Webster, John Kinyon, (son of James,) Jonathan Kinyon, James Adams, Samuel Barber, William Clark, (son of Samuel,) James Jeames, Jonathan Jeames, Nicholas Larkin, Joseph Card, Robert Lillibridge, Joseph Clarke, William Clark, Jun'r., Stephen Richmond, Samuel Perry, Jun'r., Sylvester Kinyon, Enoch Kinyon, William Bentley, Joseph Cross, John Webb, Jonathan Clark, James Congdon, Jun'r., Jeremiah Boss, William Potter, Richard Boss, Thomas Adams, Samuel Tift, William Potter, Jun'r., Thomas Clarke, Simeon Clark, Daniel Stanton, Daniel Kinyon, Peleg Cross, Enoch Kinyon, Jun'r., John Ladd, Joseph Kinyon, Benjamin Barber, Nathaniel Deelman, Nathaniel

Deelman, Jun'r., Thomas Gould, Elisha Clark, Joseph Stanton, Jun'r., William Welsh, Benjamin Clark, Israel Stiles, Joseph Dodge, Robert Austin, Joseph Woodmansie, Stephen Rose, Joseph Barber, Elisha Halls, John Halls, Joseph Woodmansie, Jun'r., John More, Ezekiel Barber, Samuel Irish, Joseph Hollway, Robert Clark, Edward Jeames, Caleb Clark, Samuel Mott, Ruben Johnson, Thomas Stanton, Daniel Stanton, Jun'r., Samuel Stanton, William Ross, Jun'r., David Austin, William Petty, William Petty, Jun'r., Benjamin Hoxsie, James Webster, William Clark, David Nichols, David More, Card Foster, Joseph Tift.

## WEST GREENWICH.

John Greene, (s. of John,) John Spencer, Samuel Hopkins, Preserved Hall, John Matteson, William Cumstock, Philip Greene, James Reynolds, (son of Fran.,) Silas Green, William Hall, Jeremiah Ellis, Ebenezer Matteson, Obediah Jencks, Henry Matteson, Jun'r., Henry Green, John Cass, Arthur Aylsworth, Henry Matteson, (s. of H. Jr,) John Austin Jr., Charles Carr, James Green, Ezekiel Whitford, John Weak, Joseph Nichols, Gideon Ellis, George Gardner, Robert Austin, Samuel Spencer, Ishmael Spink, William Hopkins, Thomas Carpenter, Thomas Strait, Jeremiah Carpenter, Jonathan Matteson, Shibne Spink, John Greene, Jun'r., (son of Jno.) Thomas Strait, (son of Jno.) Thomas Weight, Caleb Carr, (Joyner,) Sam'l. Spink, Benjamin Carr, Samuel Rogers, Joseph Reynolds, Pardon Tillinghast, Benjamin Spink, Ayres Ellis, Peter Wells, Josias Sweet, John Albro, John Tillinghast, Chaddiah Aylworth, Robert Carpenter.

## COVENTRY.

Robert Greene, Vosel Greene, Jeremiah Greene, Thomas Weltch, Thomas Matheson, James Greene, George Hall, Benjamin Gardner, Tobe Greene, Samuel Cooper, Joseph Matheson, Amos Stafford, Abel Potter, Samuel Baley, Elisha Johnson, Benjamin Nichols, John Johnson, William Burlingame, Joseph Potter, Adam Low, Joseph Weaver, John Elenton, Jun'r., Thomas Cohien, Tobe Potter, John Weekes, Mansur Cooper, John Bucklen, Thomas Nichols, Robert Havens, Thomas Stafford, Jun'r., William Nichols, Thomas Greene, Ebenezer Greene, Obediah Johnson, Charles Higingbottom, Nathan Goff, Anthony Cory, John Waterman, Samuel Cooper, Jun'r., Thomas Weltch, Jun'r., William Bates, Thomas Parker,

John Skillon, Richard Herrenton, Jun'r., Richard Stafford, Aaron Bowen, Caleb Greene, Samuel Cook, Daniel Weltch, Peleg Spencer, Isaac Howard, Bartholomew Johnson, Philip Arlsworth, Nathaniel Greene, Wardel Greene, John Nichols, John Andrew, Sandders Dixon, Mathew Roberts, Christopher Knight, Christopher Cohien, Stephen Nichols, William Stafford, Benoni Prise, Thomas Brayton, ·Randal Rice, Moses Blanshard, Jonathan Nichols, Benjamin Blanchard, Thomas Stafford, (Son W.) Daniel Greene, William Briggs, Richard Rice.

### EXETER.

Nicholas Gardner, Esq'r., Job Tripp, Esq'r., David Sprague, John Rogers, Esq'r., John Baker, Capt. Peleg Thomas, Joseph Arnold, Capt. John Reynolds, Benoni Hall, John Weight, John Potter, Michael Dawley, Isaac Gardner, Jun'r., Benoni Gardner, Isaac Gardner, Job Herrington, Jeremiah Austin, Jun'r., Benjamin Lawton, Jeremiah Gardner, Simon Smith, Job Herrington, Jun'r., Pedigreene Tripp, Joseph Potter, Jun'r., John Hall, Robert Gardner, George Reynolds, Benjamin Mory, Moses Slocum, John Rathbun, 3d, John Gardner, Jun'r., Thomas Bentley, John Champlin, Samuel Gardner, Edward Slocum, Peleg Tripp, Joseph Olin, Mitchel Case, John Gardner, William Bently, Thomas Casey, Samuel Casey, Francis Reynolds, Stephen Austin, Joseph Weight, Caleb Arnold, Thomas Lewis, Stephen Willcox, George Weight, Thomas Rathbone, Robert Aylsworth, George Codner, Daniel Barber.

### MIDDLETOWN.

Daniel Gould, James Barker, Jun'r., John Barker, Robert Barker, Thomas Coggeshall, James Coggeshall, Edward Easton, John Greene, Robert Nichols, James Philips, Peleg Peckham, Isaac Smith, Peleg Slocum, William Turner, John Tayler, Thomas Weaver, Thomas Weaver, Jun'r., Clement Weaver, Francis Weeden, John Wood, Thomas Weaver, (son of Thomas, Jun'r.,) John Allen, Samuel Allen, George Cornel, George Cornel, Jun'r., Joshua Coggeshal, Lawrence Clarke, Jun'r., Thomas Gould, Daniel Gould, Jun'r., Peleg Smith, John Pebody, James Peckham, Samuel Rogers, Peleg Rogers, John Rogers, Jeremiah Rogers, Benjamin Weaver, John Weaver, Benjamin Smith, Benjamin Weaver, Jun'r., Thomas Weaver, (son of Benjamin,) Clement Weaver, Jun'r., John Weaver, Jun'r., William Weeden, William Weeden, Jun'r., Peter Easton, Walter Easton, Sam'l. Bailey.

## BRISTOL.

Samuel Smith, Thomas Throope, Joseph Reynolds, John Throope, Nathaniel Bosworth, Hopestil Potter, John Dyre, Elisha May, Thomas Throope, Jun'r., Jeremiah Finney, Maj'r. Thomas Greene, William Gallap, Samuel Vial, Esq'r., Cornelius Waldron, John Walker, Jeremiah Dimon, Rogers Richmond, John Bushee, Timothy Ingraham, Joseph Russel, Esq'r., George Dunbar, Esq'r., William Pearse, Nathaniel Pearse, Benjamin Reynolds, Joshua Baly, Isaac Lawton, Jonathan Woodberry, Esq'r., Capt. Thomas Lawton, Joseph Eddy, John Lindzey, Nathaniel Munro, Ebenezer Dyre, John Throope, Jun'r., Benjamin Smith, Joseph Wardwell, Benjamin Salsbury, John Howland, William Hoar, William Coggeshall, Samuel Howland, Thomas Weaver, Elisha Weaver, Henry Bragg, William Bosworth, Joseph Reynolds, Jun'r., Jonathan Peck, Esq'r., Simeon Munro, John May, Thomas Munro, Jo'n. Bosworth, Jun'r., William Coggeshall, Jun'r., Thomas Kinnicut, Nathaniel Fales, John Wardwell, Joseph Waldron, John Hubbard, James Bosworth, Joshua Ingraham, Bennet Munro, John Munro, John Oldridge, Aaron Bourn, Samuel Bosworth, Joseph Waldron, Jun'r., Nathaniel Cary, Capt. Samuel Woodberry, James Wardwell, Thomas Jolls, John Coy, Simeon Potter, Joseph Phillips, Josiah Howland, William Munro, John Bosworth, John Peck, Capt. Samuel Gallap.

### TIVERTON.

John Manchester, Esq'r., William Almy, Samuel Snell, Sen'r., Joseph Anthony, Roger Cory, Capt. Thomas Cook, Thomas Weight, Edward Wanton, John Borden, Samuel Hix, Samuel Durfey, Weston Hix, Stephen Cook, Thomas Howland, John Taber, Ephraim Willcox, Cornelius Soul, Philip Cory, Thomas Cook (son of Joseph) George Cook, William Willcock, John Almy, Ebenezer Taber, John Bennet. Benjamin Durfie, Peter Talman, John Jennings, Abraham Barker, Samuel Borden, Restcome Sanford, Oliver Bealy, Samuel Snell, Jun'r., Joseph Tabor, John Tabor (son of John,) Samuel Hart, Jonathan Hart, William Sanford, Thomas Weight, Jun'r., Peleg Sanford, Joshua Dwelly, Sen'r., Joshua Dwelly Jun'r., Blake Perry, John Cook, (son of Thomas,) William Woddle, John Bowen, Samuel Shearman, William Shrieve, William Fish, John Sisson, William Manchester, (son of Stephen,)

Joseph Crandal, Josiah Sawyer, David Lake, Joseph Jennings, Thomas Mosher, Benjamin Macomber, Philip Tabor, Joseph Tabor, (son of Philip,) Benjamin Chase, Jun'r., William Cook, Thomas Fish, William Cory, Jonathan Davel, Isaac Howland, George Westgate, Benjamin Brayton, Thomas Anthony, Caleb Cory, Philip Gray, Thomas Gray, Edward Gray, William Gray, John Brown, Thomas Willcock, Joseph Wanton, John Cook, Capt. John Pearce, Benjamin Chace, Peleg Shearman, Peter Davel, Daniel Earl, David Durfy, Samuel Hart, Jun'r., Smiton Hart, Capt. Job Durfie, Joseph Stafford, David Stafford, Christopher Davel, Abraham Stafford, Israel Davel, Abner Chase, Josiah Willcock, Giles Brownel, William Springer, Gershom Woddel, Richard Tripp, James Weeden, Thomas Cook, (son of John Cook.)

## LITTLE COMPTON.

Capt. John Palmer, William Richmond, Esq'r., Samuel Gray, Caleb Church, William Simmons, Nathaniel Searls, Jun'r., Henry Wood, George Rouse, Silvester Wodman, William Davis, Richard Heart, Jos., Peckham, Robert Woodman, Samuel Tompkins, James Peirce, Benjamin Simmonds, Samuel Willbur, Esq'r., George Pearce, Robert Carr, William Grinell, Richard Grinell, John Tompson, Enos Gifford, William Simmonds, Jun'r., Edward Irish, Samuel Cook, Joseph Tompkins, Henry Wood, Jun'r., Jeptha Pearce, William Pearce, Elisha Clap, William Hall, Esq'r., Robert Taylor, Esq'r, Capt. John Hunt, Capt. Thomas Brownel, Isaac Willbur, Joseph Briggs, Thomas Burgess, Lemuel Shaw, Walter Wilbur, Jeremiah Briggs, John Willbur, Constant Southworth, John Taylor, Jun'r., Thomas Stoddard, John Willbur, Jun'r., Joseph Wood, William Shaw, Joseph Davenport, William Willbur, William Willbur, Jun'r., John Brownel, Elisha Woodworth, Elihu Woodworth, William Briggs, Joseph Willbur, Thomas Willbur, Joseph Coe, Jeremiah Brownel, Anthony Shaw, John Gifford, John Palmer, Jun'r., John Pabodie, Jeremiah Shaw, Charles Brownel, Oliver Hillard, John Wood, William Briggs, Jun'r., Edward Burgess, Joseph Willbur, Jun'r., Peter Shaw, Benjamin Church, Thomas Palmer, Samuel Baley, John Baley, Benjamin Shaw, Joseph Burgess, Richard Brownel, George Baley, George Peirce, Jun'r., William Head, Febes Little, Thomas Brownel, (son of Robert,) Peter Taylor, Joseph Palmer, John Baley, Jun'r., William Head, Jun'r., John Horswell, William Hunt, John Irish, Benjamin Seabury, William Tayler, Stephen Hart.

## WARREN.

Mathew Allen, Esq'r, Peleg Heath, Capt. Samuel Miller, Ebenezer Allen, Nathaniel Peck, James Smith, Josiah Humphrey, John Adams, Benjamin Miller, Walter Heril, Joseph Allen, 2d, Elijah Rawson, Ebenezer Garnsey, Capt. Joseph Allen, Joseph Allen, Jun'r., John Kinnicut, Capt. James Mason, William Eastabroke, John Eastabroke, Samuel Humphry, Ebenezer Cole, Benjamin Cole, Nathan Miller, Joseph Butterworth, Caleb Carr, Solomon Peck, Samuel Barns, Samuel Low, James Brown, Elder Joseph Mason, Ebenezer Adams, Joseph Vial, Daniel Peck, Samuel Allen, Ebenezer Allen, Jun'r., Capt. Barnard Heril, Barnard Heril, Jun'r., Hucker Low, Caleb Eddy, John Mason, Mathew Watson, Joseph Mason, Esq'r, Benja. Barton, Isaac Wheaton, John Wheaton, Josiah Bowen, John Cole, Jun'r., Oliver Salsbury, Joshua Smith, Benjamin Smith, Richard Thomas, Benjamin Drown, John Eastabroke, Jun'r., John Luther, Philip Short, James Bowen, Jonas Humphry, Benjamin Butterworth, Edward Luther, John Butterworth, William Salsbury, Edward Bosworth, Samuel Miller, Jun'r., Josiah Humphry, Jun'r., John Kelley, John Child, John Martin, Nathaniel Eastabroke, Nathaniel Bowen, Samuel Bowen, Constant Vial, Josiah Kent, Joseph Grant, Ebenezer Martin, Joshua Bicknal, Jun'r., Amos Thomas, Israel Peck, Ebenezer Luther, William Knowles, Ephraim Tiffany, Thomas Cole, Joshua Bicknel.

## CUMBERLAND.

Joseph Brown, James Ballou, Nathaniel Ballou, Obediah Ballow, Josiah Cook, Samuel Bartlet, Job Bartlet, William Walcot, Daniel Peck, Janiel Jencks, Jacob Bartlet, Jun'r., Nathan Jillson, Jun'r., Joseph Staples, John Bartlet, Jeremiah Bartlet, Israel Whipple, Gideon Tower, Daniel Wilkinson, Richard Aldrich, Daniel Whipple, Jeremiah Wilkinson, Joshua Hall, Daniel Smith, David Whipple, Jeremiah Whipple, Richard Darling, Benjamin Race, Edward Smith, David Race, Benja. Brown, John Grant, Richard Esties, William Carpenter, John Dexter, Gideon Bishop, Benja. Brown, Jun'r., Peter Whipple, Samuel Whipple, Benja. Tower, Daniel Whipple, Jun'r., Joseph Raze, Joseph Brown, Jun'r., William Walcot, Jun'r., John Bishop, Joseph Whipple, Stephen Sprague, Solomon Aldrich, John Cass, Nathaniel Cook, Uriah Tillson, John Tower, Ichabod

3

Peck, Banfield Capron, Elisha Newel, Peter Darling, Ariah Ballou, Ezekiel Ballou, Amiiah Ballow, Ichabod Peck, Jun'r., Daniel Peck, Jun'r., Richard Aldrich, Jun'r., Benjamin Davie, Ebenezer Barras, Jun'r., Noah Bartlet, Jun'r., Francis Inman, Stephen Brown, Jonathan Armsby, Jeremiah Inman, David Hogg.

## TUESDAY, MAY 3d, 1748.

The persons, whose names here follow, having taken the oath or affirmation prescribed by the law of this colony against bribery and corruption, are hereby admitted to give their votes to choose officers for their respective towns, and also to give their votes for the choice of the general officers of the colony :—

### NEWPORT.

Henry Bull, John Clarke, (mariner,) Elisha Gibbs, William Dyre, Caleb Godfrey, Mathias King, Joseph Stacey, Thomas Borden, Moses Pitman, Jonathan Sabin, Jahleel Brenton, Ebenezer Flagg, William Weeden, William James, John Dennis, (mariner,) Barnabas Hargell, Oliver Child, Cuthbert Campbell, Ebenezer Davenport, William Mumford, Charles Wickham, Nathaniel Coddington, Samuel Tillinghast, Henry Stacey, John Bristow, Pardon Tillinghast, William Lake, John Rouse, William Stoddard, John Goddard, James Cahoone, Joseph Carrier, Israel Brayton, John Thurston, (son of Jonathan,) James Rogers, John Coddington, George Shearman, Joseph Bull, Robert Gibbs, William Pinnegar, Solomon Townsend, John Jepson, James Hastings, Edward Wanton, Richard Ward, John Freebody, David Cheseborough, Daniel Russel, Eleaser Trivet, Handley Chipman, Francis Sandford, Caleb Arnold, William Clagget, Jun'r., Henry Tisdale, Josiah Brown, William Hoockey, Jonathan Jeffers, Samuel Dyre, Henry Coggeshall, Henry Stevenson, William Clarke, John Warren, (son of Joseph,) Lewis Sayer, Nathaniel Chapman, John Tweedy, John Sandford, John Easton, (son of Samuel,) Clarke Brown, William Strengthfield, Jonathan Bardin, James Holmes, John Holmes Gardner, Godfrey Mallbone, Jun'r., Robert Feeke, John James, (caulker,) John Brown, William Weeden, Stephen

Hoockey, Ralph Stanhope, Solomon Senter, John Bazzin, Clothier Peirce, Jun'r., Nathan Townend, John Bryer, William Arnold, James Leach, Southcote Langworthy, David Melvil, William Brenton, Job Townsend, Jun'r., Joseph Gladding, Samuel Brown, Pollipus Hammond.

## PROVIDENCE.

Arthur Fenner, Benjamin Eddy, William Harris, Richard Knight, William Olney, Solomon Drown, Jonathan Whipple, Nathaniel Wateman, Roger Kinnicut, Edward Arnold, Joseph Crawford, Charles Dyre, John Dyre, Joseph Randal, Jun'r., William Dyre, Samuel Westcot, Jun'r., John Hoyle, John Knight, Jacob Hartshorn, John Hawkins, David Roberts, Jonathan Bucklin, Daniel Burlingame, Charles Atwood, Stephen Olney, Arthur Fenner, Jun'r., John Manton, Samuel Ladd, Jun'r., Gideon Cumstock, and Paul Tew.

## PORTSMOUTH.

Joseph Brownel, Jun'r., Roger Burrington, Thomas Lawton, Caleb Shrieve, Robert Burrington, Job Almy, John Fish, John Burrington, George Sisson, William Allen, (son of John,) Jonathan Allen, Clark Cornel, Samuel Albro, Jun'r., Nathan Chase, Benjamin Lawton, Daniel Lake, Henry Brightman, Joseph Ward, Thomas Cory, John Cory, Joseph Brownel, Abiel Tripp, John Coggeshall, William Hall, Jun'r., David Fish, and John Allen.

## WARWICK.

William Utter, William Gorton, Samuel Pearce, Rowland Barton, Azickam Pearce, Benjamin Tiffany, Thomas Green, Stephen Green, Michael Levalley, Samuel Green, Jun'r., Stephen Colegrove, Jun'r., Samuel Warner, Stephen Scranton, Thomas Wickes, Benjamin Wickes, Thomas Wickes, Elisha Green, Jun'r., Philip Arnold, Jun'r., Andrew Edmunds, Joseph Hedley, and Stukely Stafford.

## WESTERLY.

Elias Thompson, Edward Saunders, Jun'r., Thomas Wells, Eleazer Brown, John Mackoon, Jun'r., Joseph Crumb, John Mackcarter, Joseph Mackcoon, Sephen Willcox, Caleb Church,

Zaccheus Runnolds, Edward Wells, Edward Wells, Jun'r., Nathan Babcock, Jun'r., James Bleavin, Ezekiel Burdick, James Wells, Joseph Runnolds, Hubbard Burdick, (son to Hubbard,) James Saunders, John Maxson, (son to John Maxson, Jun'r.,) James Clarke, and Ichabod Clarke.

## NEW SHOREHAM.

Edward Sands, Robert Hull, John Littlefield, Abel Franklin, Thomas Dickens, Samuel Rathbun, John Pain, Thomas Pain, John Ball, John Mott, Edward Ball, John Dodge, Jonathan Mitchel, John Rathbun, Thomas Mitchel, Daniel Rose, Caleb Littlefield, Nathaniel Littlefield, Stephen Franklin, Joseph Mitchel, Jun'r., William Dodge, Samuel Dodge, and Nathaniel Mott.

## NORTH KINGSTOWN.

John Spink, Jonathan Allen, Joshua Green, William Congdon, Peter Rennolds, Jun'r., Joseph Smith, Samuel Phillips, Nicholas Northup, Jun'r., Samuel Eldred, Nathaniel Havens, William Havens, William Hall, John Brown, George Wightman, Jun'r., Samuel Boone, Joseph Corey, Samuel Warner, George Fowler, George Nichols, Nathaniel Carpenter, Samuel Albro, Samuel Ellis, Samuel Watson, Jeremiah Baker, Alexander Havens, John Bissel, Samuel Rathbun, George Wightman, Hutchinson Clark, and Alexander Huling, Jun'r.

## SOUTH KINGSTOWN.

Thomas Taylor, Samuel Gardner, William Hull, Jireh Mumford, Sylvanus Greenman, Henry Gardner, Benedict Helme, John Sheldon, (son of Isaac,) William Knowles, Peter Boss, John Smith, Jun'r., Alexander Case, John Brown, Hezekiah Babcock, John Smith, Thomas Gardner, Oliver Haszard, Samuel Willson, Ephraim Smith, Latham Clarke, and Nathaniel Perkins.

## EAST GREENWICH.

Joseph Bealey, Peleg Spencer, William Sweet, Walter Spencer, Thomas Fry, Thomas Nichols, (son of James,) Thomas Aldrich, Robert Whitford, Thomas Aldrich, Michael Spencer, (son of Abner,)

Thomas Nichols, (the third,) Duty Jarald, Charles Andrew, Josiah Jones, Thomas Nichols, (son of Thomas, Jun'r.,) Daniel Mattison, and Joseph Stafford.

### JAMESTOWN.

John Eldred, Matthew Grinnold, John Hull, and James Carr.

### SMITHFIELD.

John Dexter, Leonard Smith, John Sayles, Joseph Smith, (the third) Richard Harris, Jeremiah Mowry, Benjamin Pain, John Ballow, Joseph Smith, William Bates, Thomas Beadle, Nathan Staples, Israel Wilkinson, Joseph Herrenden, Jun'r., Peter Barns, Robert Latham, Preserved Harris, John Sayles, Jun'r., Peter Ballow, Jun'r., Uriah Arnold, John Malavery, Valentine Whiteman, Jun'r., Job Angel, Daniel Cumstock, Jun'r., Elijah Cook, Henry Blackman, Sylvanus Sayles, Thomas Herrenden, Stephen Sly, Elisha Arnold, Samuel Aldrich, Jun'r., William Olney, Caleb Arnold, Job Arnold, Jonathan Harris, Benjamin Cook, William Brown, Thomas Arnold, John Man, Jun'r., Elisha Mowrey, Daniel Sayles, Richard Arnold, Ebenezer Cass, Oliver Mowrey, Samuel Aldrich, and Daniel Cumstock.

### SCITUATE.

Amos Hopkins, Henry Randal, Jun'r., William Hammon, James Thornton, John Smith, Joseph Weatherhead, Ezekiel Hopkins, Jun'r., Joseph Tucker, Oziel Hopkins, Stephen Wilbore, Charles Hopkins, Ezekiel Hopkins, John Taylor, John Herrenden, Eliza Collins Jun'r., William Sheldon, Thomas Barns, Nehemiah Angell, Chodd Aylsworth, David Sprague, Joshua Angell, Amos Hammon, William Salsbury, Isaiah Angell. George Stone, Fisher Potter, Jonathan Mowry, Jonathan Cole, Nathan Bates, Joseph Kimbel, Josiah Herrenden, Joseph Guile, Benjamin Bennet, Jonathan Bennet, John Howland, Joseph Hopkins, Simon Davis, Robert Whitman, Thomas Realph, John Weight, Job Shippee, Christopher Realph, George Wilbour, Jonathan Pray, John Seamons, Samuel Wilkinson, Thomas Colins, William Seamons, Timothy Hopkins, Josiah Bennet, Henry Whitman, Joseph Wilkinson, Alexander Lovel, William Corey, Richard Calwell, John Lovel, and Samuel Perkins.

## GLOCESTER.

Stephen Inman, Zachariah Jencks, Job Phetteplace, Stephen Smith, Robert Smith, Joseph Winsor, Abraham Smith, Elisha Herrenden, William Herrenden, John Whipple, and Edward Bishop.

## CHARLESTOWN.

Daniel Peckham, Thomas Kinyon, Joseph Johnson, John Millard, John Halls, Jun'r., Peter Halls, Nathaniel Lewis, John Congdon, and Daniel Peckham, Jun'r.

## WEST GREENWICH.

Daniel Hill, Jun'r., Hezekiah Matteson, (son of Henry,) Joshua Gardner, Pasca Whitford, Thomas Joslin, John Green, Nicholas Whitford, Abraham Mattison, David Whitford, Isaac Johnson, Griffen Sweet, Samuel Reynolds, Harris Weaver, William Sweet, John Weaver, Elisha Weaver, Christopher Hall, John Hopkins, John Gardner, John Cass, Jun'r., Thomas Cumstock, Samuel Niles, Joseph Dolliver, John Reynolds, (son of Samuel,) and Benjamin Rogers.

## COVENTRY.

Caleb Colven, Benjamin Gorton, Josias Colven, Adam Casson, Francis Brayton, Ephraim Tingley, Joseph Tillinghast, Daniel Cummins, Jonathan Nichols, (son of Richard,) Ichabod Potter, Charles Andrew, and John Lee.

## EXETER.

Thomas Gardner, Robert Moon, James Moon, Samuel Eldred, Philip Green, John James, Samuel Weight, John Dawley, John Albro, Benjamin Potter, Samuel Dawley, John Rathbun, William Sunderlin, Jeffery Champlin, Joseph Rathbun, Joseph Rathbun, Jun'r., Nathan Dawley, John Sweet, William Eldred, Samuel Baker, Robert Sweet, James Nichols, John Colegrove, and Jeffry Wilcox.

## MIDDLETOWN.

Nicholas Brown, James Barker, Edward Tew, Cornelius Clarke, Robert Lawton, William Barker, Joshua Coggeshall, (son of James,)

James Barker, (son of James, Jun'r.,) Lawrence Clarke, William Peckham, Samuel Peckham, William Peckham, Jun'r., Jeremiah Barker, William Wood, William Brown, William Barker, Samuel Rogers, Jun'r., William Lawton, Joshua Coggeshall, (son of James,) and Robert Lawton.

## BRISTOL.

Mark Anthony D'Woolf, John Raynolds, Daniel Bradford, Samuel Clark, Isaac Wheaton, John Gladding, Jun'r., William Oldrig, Jeremiah Bosworth, Michael Phillips, Jonathan Woodberry, Jun'r., William Lindsey, James Gibbs, and Henry Bragg.

## TIVERTON.

John Manchester, Esq'r., Samuel Snell, Joseph Anthony, Roger Cory, Thomas Cook, Thomas Weight, Edward Wanton, John Bordon, Samuel Hix, Samuel Durfie, Weston Hix, Stephen Cook, Thomas Howland, John Taber, Ephraim Wilcock, John Almy, Ebenezer Taber, Cornelius Soule, Philip Cory, Thomas Cook, (son of Joseph,) George Cook, William Wilcock, John Bennit, Benjamin Durfie, Peter Talman, John Jennings, Abraham Barker, Samuel Borden, Restcome Sanford, Oliver Bealey, Samuel Snell, Jun'r., Joseph Taber, John Taber, (son of John,) Samuel Hart, Jonathan Hart, William Sandford, Thomas Weight, Jun'r., Peleg Sandford, Joshua Dwelly, Blake Peary, John Cook, (son of Thomas,) Thomas Mosher, William Woodle, John Bowen, Samuel Sherman, William Shrieve, William Fish, William Manchester, (son of Stephen,) Josiah Sawyer, David Lake, Joseph Jenning, Benjamin Macomber, Philip Taber, Joseph Taber, (son of Philip,) Benjamin Chase, Jun'r., William Fisk, Thomas Fish, William Cory, Jonathan Davel, Isaac Howland, George Westgate, Benjamin Brayton, Thomas Anthony, Caleb Cory, Philip Gray, Thomas Gray, Edward Gray, William Gray, John Brown, Thomas Wilcock, Joshua Dwelly, Jun'r., Joseph Wanton, John Cook, John Pearce, Benjamin Chase, Peter Davel, Daniel Earl, David Durfie, Samuel Hart, Jun'r., Smiton Hart, Job Durfie, Joseph Stafford, David Stafford, Abraham Stafford, Abner Chase, Josiah Wilcock, Giles Brownel, William Springer, Gershom Woddel, Richard Tripp, James Weeden, Thomas Cook, (son of John Cook,) Joseph Seaberry, Samuel Almy, Thomas Crandal, Paul Taber, Benjamin Hambly, Job Almy, William Manchester, (son of John,) Daniel Earl, Jun'r., John Sawyer, Oliver Cook, and John Thomas.

## LITTLE COMPTON.

John Palmer, William Richmond, Samuel Gray, Caleb Church, William Simmons, Nathaniel Searls, Jun'r., Henry Wood, George Rouse, Silvester Woodman, William Davis, Richard Hart, Joseph Peckcom, Robert Woodman, Samuel Tomkins, James Pearce, Benjamin Simmous, Samuel Wilbor, George Pearce, Robert Carr, William Grinell, Richard Grinell, Elisha Clap, Enos Gifford, William Simmons, Jun'r., Edward Irish, Samuel Cook, Joseph Tomkins, Henry Wood, Jun'r., Jeptha Pierce, William Pierce, John Palmer, Jun'r., John Price, Thomas Baley, John Brownel, (son of Margaret,) William Price, John Simmons, (son of Joseph,) William Hall, Robert Taylor, John Hunt, Thomas Brownel, Isaac Wilbor, Joseph Briggs, Thomas Burgess, Lemuel Shaw, Walter Wilbor, Jeremiah Briggs, Jonathan Brownel, Constant Southwarth, John Taylor, Thomas Stoddard, Henry Head, Joseph Wood, William Shaw, Joseph Davenport, William Wilbor, William Wilbor, (son of Samuel,) John Brownel, Elisha Woodwarth, Elihu Woodwarth, William Briggs, Joseph Wilbor, Thomas Wilbor, Joseph Coe, Jeremiah Brownel, Anthony Shaw, John Gifford, Stephen Hart, Joseph Simmons, John Woodman, Samuel Gray, Jun'r., Daniel Grinell, John Pabodie, Jeremiah Shaw, Charles Brownel, Oliver Hillard, John Wood, William Briggs, (son of Job,) Silvester Palmer, Joseph Wilbor, (son of William,) Peter Shaw, Benjamin Church, Thomas Palmer, Samuel Baley, John Baley, Benjamin Shaw, Joseph Burgess, Richard Brownel, George Baley, George Pierce, Jun'r., William Head, Fobes Little, Thomas Little, (son of Robert,) Peter Taylor, Joseph Palmer, John Baley, (son of William,) William Head, (son of Henry,) John Horswell, William Hunt, John Irish, Benjamin Seabury, William Taylor, John Irish, (son of David,) John Shrieve, Edward Church, Job Hunt, and Aaron Wilbor.


## WARREN.

Mathew Allen, Peleg Heath, Ebenezer Allen, Nathaniel Peck, James Smith, Josiah Humphrey, John Adams, Benjamin Miller, Walter Hail, Joseph Allen, (the second,) Elijah Rawson, Ebenezer Garnsey, John Kinnicut, James Mason, William Eastabroke, John Eastabroke, Ebenezer Cole, Benjamin Cole, Nathan Miller, Joseph Butterworth, Caleb Carr, Solomon Peck, Samuel Barns, Samuel

Low, James Brown, Joseph Maxon, Ebenezer Adams, Joseph Vial, Daniel Peck, Samuel Allen, Ebenezer Allen, Jun'r., Barnard Hail, Barnard Hail, Jun'r., Hooker Low, Caleb Eddy, John Mason, Mathew Watson, Benjamin Barton, John Wheaton, John Cole, Jun'r., Oliver Salsbury, Joshua Smith, Benjamin Smith, Richard Thomas, Benjamin Drown, John Eastabroke, (the second,) John Luther, Philip Short, James Bowen, Jonas Humphry, Benjamin Butterworth, Edward Luther, John Butterworth, William Salsbury, Edward Bosworth, Samuel Miller, Jun'r., Josiah Humphry, Jun'r., John Kelly, John Child, John Martin, Nathaniel Eastabroke, Nathaniel Bowen, Samuel Bowen, Constant Vial, Josiah Kent, Joseph Grant, Ebenezer Martin, Joshua Bicknal, Joshua Bicknal, Jun'r., Amos Thomas, Israel Peck, Thomas Cole, Ebenezer Luther, Ephraim Tiffany, Thomas Barns, Ebenezer Luther, Jun'r., Richard Hail, Hezekiah Tiffany, John Allen, Richard Bullock and Robert Eastabroke.

## CUMBERLAND.

Joseph Brown, James Ballow, Obediah Ballow, Josiah Cook, Samuel Bartlet, Job Bartlet, William Wallcot, Daniel Peck, Daniel Jencks, Nathaniel Jilson, Jun'r., Joseph Staples, John Bartlet, Jeremiah Bartlet, Israel Whipple, Gideon Tower, Daniel Wilkinson, Richard Aldrich, Daniel Whipple, Jeremiah Wilkinson, Joshua Hall, Daniel Smith, David Whipple, Jeremiah Whipple, Richard Darling, Benjamin Raze, Edward Smith, David Raze, Benjamin Brown, John Grant, Richard Esties, William Carpenter, John Dexter, Gideon Bishop, Benjamin Brown, Jun'r., Peter Whipple, Samuel Whipple, Benjamin Tower, Daniel Whipple, Jun'r., Joseph Raze, Joseph Brown, Jun'r., William Wallcot, Jun'r., John Bishop, Joseph Whipple, Stephen Sprague, Solomon Aldrich, John Cass, Nathaniel Cook, Uriah Jillson, John Tower, Ichabod Peck, Banfield Capron, Elisha Newel, Peter Darling, Arial Ballow, Ezekiel Ballow, Amriah Ballow, Ichabod Peck, Jun'r., Daniel Peck, Jun'r., Richard Aldrich, Jun'r., Benjamin Davel, Ebenezer Barras, Jun'r., Noah Bartlet, Jun'r., Francis Inman, Stephen Brown, Jonathan Armsby, Jeremiah Inman, David Hogg, Jonathan Sprague, John Whipple, Ichabod Bosworth, Abraham Barras, Charles Capron, and Daniel Weatherhead.

4

### RICHMOND.

John Stanton, David Kinyon, John Bentley, David Kinyon, Jun'r., John Tanner, John Teft, Thomas Rogers, Oliver Mins, Simeon Watson, Robert Moor, and John Enoss, Jun'r.

## TUESDAY, MAY 2d, 1749.

The persons whose names hereafter follow, having taken the oath or affirmation prescribed by the law of this colony against bribery and corruption, are hereby admitted to give their votes to choose officers for their respective towns, and also to give their votes for the choice of the general officers of the colony.

### NEWPORT.

William Redwood, Benjamin Johnson, Joseph Rider, John Banister, Charles Bardin, David Moore, George Gardner, Ephraim Harris, Jonathan Clarke, James Perrin, Samuel Easton, Andrew Hunter, Henry Tisdale, Benjamin Ellery, James Gardner, William Gardner, Samuel Marryot, Zebulon Spinney, Daniel Russell, Jun'r., Solomon Senter, Thomas Creapman, John Spooner, Charles Dyre, Timothy Hill, John Whiting, Simeon Price, Robert Robinson, Benoni Gardner, and Joseph Turner.

### PROVIDENCE.

Jonathan Sheldon, David Wilkinson, Joshua Turner, Richard Brown, Nicholas Cooke, Samuel Congdon, Benjamin Cary, Caleb Potter, Edward Arnold, Richard Bowen, John Field, Jun'r., William Dean, Rufus Hopkins, William Antram, Jun'r., Jonathan Jencks, Peter Burlingame, Jun'r., Zephaniah Peck, William Smith, George Laws, Daniel Olney, Joseph Hawkins, Joseph Waterman, Jun'r., Richard Smith, Thomas Birkit, John Burlingame, Jun'r., Jacob Whitman, Joshua Turner, Jun'r., Benjamin Whipple, Jun'r., Gideon Manchester, Oliver Angel, Asaph Bowen, Gideon Smith, and William Carpenter, (son of William.)

## PORTSMOUTH.

Caleb Allen, Samuel Albro. Michael Cory, George Shearman, John Allen, Jun'r., Joseph Shearman, Thomas Sisson, Robert Dennis, John Lawton, (son of Joseph.) and Enoch Butts.

## WARWICK.

George Wightman, John Wightman, Jun'r., John Green, (son of Richard,) Thomas Price, Matthew Price, Ebenezer Green, Daniel Budlong, Joseph Wickes, and Ebenezer King.

## WESTERLY.

Christopher Sugar, Ichabod Prosser, Benjamin Brown. William Burdick, Thomas Burdick, Nicholas Vincent, and Oliver Chase.

## NEW SHOREHAM.

Edward Sands, Robert Hull, John Dodge. Nathaniel Littlefield, Stephen Franklin, John Rathburn. Thomas Pain, John Pain, Jonathan Mitchel, Joseph Mitchel. Thomas Mitchel, Joseph Mitchel, Jun'r., Edward Ball, Thomas Dickens, William Dodge, Samuel Dodge, Abel Franklin, Daniel Rose. John Mott, Nathaniel Mott, John Ball, Caleb Littlefield, John Littlefield, Samuel Rathburn, and Samuel Champlin.

## NORTH KINGSTOWN.

Peter Reynolds Jun'r., William Hall, (son of John,) Benjamin Cole, Samuel Boone, John Allen, William Clarke, Philip Card, Peleg Card, Henry Spencer, Thomas Bissel, Thomas Havens, Samuel Shearman, Edward Gardner, Jeremiah Smith, and John Wightman.

## SOUTH KINGSTOWN.

Latham Clarke, Benjamin Potter, Nicholas Watson, Ebenezer Tefft, James Shearman, Robert Potter, Jun'r., and Joseph Congdon.

## EAST GREENWICH.

Jeremiah Pain, Jun'r., John Gifford, John Manchester, Yelverton Gifford, Isaac Gardner, John Gifford, Daniel Howland, Jun'r.,

Thomas Shippey, James Fowler, David Vaughan, (son of Robert,) Nicholas Goddard, John Andrew, (son of Benoni,) and Colonel Carpenter.

### JAMESTOWN.

Benjamin Carr, (son of Thomas,) and Benjamin Sheffield.

### SMITHFIELD.

William Sprague, Richard Sayles, Jun'r., Samuel Aldrich, (the 3d,) Thomas Shippy, Jun'r., Daniel Smith, (son of William,) Samuel Bayley, Amos Arnold, William Whipple, Jun'r., Joseph Carpenter, Azariah Cumstock, John Smith, Jun'r., Jeremiah Arnold, Jun'r., Thomas Smith, Hezekiah Steere, Christopher Brown, Jeremiah Harris and Job Potter.

### SCITUATE.

Thomas Hudson, Thomas Bennet, Jun'r., Thomas Brown, Obadiah Jencks, David Young, Samuel Robins, Benjamin Weight, Jun'r., Oliver Perkins, Thomas Collins, Jun'r., Thomas Lee, and Thomas Aylsworth.

### GLOCESTER.

Joseph Olney, John Blackman, Anthony Sprague, Thomas Barns, and Isaac Richardson.

### CHARLESTOWN.

Jonathan Kinyon, Jun'r., Jeremiah Worden, Joshua Card, and John Hox.

### WEST GREENWICH.

James Reynolds, Amos Matteson, James Matteson, Christopher Carpenter, Joseph Matteson, Charles Andrew, Tibets Hopkins, James Hopkins, David Hopkins, James Willson, Robert Willson, William Willson, Joseph Niles, and Thomas Draper.

### COVENTRY.

Amos Stafford, Jun'r., Archibald Dickson, Francis Bates, Henry Green, and Robert Havens, Jun'r.

## EXETER.

Newman Perkins, William Tripp, Daniel Dawley, John Casey, William Tanner, Joseph Tanner, Benjamin Bently, and Robert Hill.

## MIDDLETOWN.

Jonathan Easton, and Thomas Durfey.

## BRISTOL.

Shearjashub Bourn, and Thomas Church.

## TIVERTON.

John Manchester, Samuel Snell, Joseph Anthony, Roger Cory, Thomas Cook, Thomas Wait, Edward Wanton, John Borden, Samuel Hicks, Samuel Durfee, Weston Hicks, Stephen Cook, Thomas Howand, John Taber, Ephraim Willcock, Cornelius Sowle, Philip Gray, Thomas Cook, (son of Joseph,) George Cook, William Willcock, John Almy, Philip Cory, Ebenezer Taber, John Bennet, Benjamin Durfee, Peter Tallman, John Jennings, Abraham Barker, Samuel Borden, Restcome Sandford, Oliver Bealy, Samuel Snell, Jun'r., Joseph Taber, John Taber, (son of John,) Samuel Hart, Jonathan Hart, William Sandford, Thomas Wait, Jun'r., Peleg Sandford, Joshua Dwelly, Joshua Dwelly, Jun'r., Blake Perry, John Cook, (son of Thomas,) William Woddle, John Bowen, Samuel Shearman, William Shreve, William Fish, William Manchester, (son of Stephen,) Joseph Crandal, Josiah Sawyer, David Lake, Joseph Jennings, Thomas Mosher, Benjamin Maccomber, Philip Taber, Joseph Taber, (son of Philip,) Benjamin Chase, Jun'r., William Cook, Thomas Fish, William Cory, Jonathan Davel, Isaac Howland, George Westgate, Thomas Anthony, Caleb Cory, Thomas Gray, Edward Gray, William Gray, John Brown, Thomas Willcock, Joseph Wanton, David Durfee, John Cook, Samuel Hart, Jun'r., Abner Chase, John Pearce, Smiton Hart, Josiah Wilcock, Benjamin Chase, Job Durfee, Giles Brownel, Peleg Shearman, Joseph Stafford, William Springer, David Stafford, Gershom Woddel, Daniel Earl, Abraham Stafford, James Weeden, Thomas Cook, (son of John,) Joseph Seabury, Samuel Almy, Thomas Crandal, Paul Taber,

Benjamin Hambly, Job Almy, William Manchester, (son of John,) Daniel Earl, Jun'r., John Sawyer, Oliver Cook, John Thomas, Ebenezer Shearman, and Noah Davenport.

### WARREN.

Peter Bicknal, Samuel Thurber, Daniel Cole, Cromwell Child, Jonathan Bosworth, Martin Luther, and William Wood.

### CUMBERLAND.

John Finney, John Nicholson, Charles Bartlet, David Dexter, Joseph Brown, (the 3d,) Joshua Hall, Jun'r., Robert Aldrich, James Dexter, Richard Stratten, Abraham Hogg, John Knox, James Rogers, Daniel Rogers, Josiah Fisk, Abiel Brown, James Ballow, Jun'r., Abraham Cook, Hezekiah Cook, and George Shearman.

### RICHMOND.

William Wilcox, Isaac Lewis, and David Potter.

### TUESDAY, MAY 1st, 1750.

It is voted and resolved, That all and every of the persons whose names hereafter follow, having taken the oath or affirmation prescribed by the law of this colony, against bribery and corruption be, and they are hereby admitted to give their votes to choose officers for the respective towns; and also to give their votes for the choice of the general officers of the colony.

### NEWPORT.

James Easton, Clothier Pearce, Christopher Bennet, Gideon Sisson, Joseph Jacob, Daniel Amory, Daniel Ayrault, Benjamin Almy, John M'quellam, Jonathan Thurston, Samuel Thurston, (son of Edward,) Israel Brayton, William Redwood, Ebenezer Davenport, Jun'r., Aaron Sheffield, John Thurston, (Taylor), John

Harris, John Rider, Thomas Rodman, John Chadwick, Christopher Hargill, Jonathan Barney, John Jepson, John King, Jacob Wilkey William James, (son of John,) Benjamin Borden, Daniel Coggeshall, Benjamin Johnson, Edward Church, Peleg Cranston, Joseph Tillinghast, John Proud, Joseph Proud, James Green, John Clarke, (blacksmith,) Walter Rodman, Edward Belcher and Samuel Greene.

### PROVIDENCE.

Nathan Pearce, Joseph Turpin, Bazzillai Richmond, Benoni Williams, Peleg Dexter, Philip Roberts, Jonathan Burlingame, Samuel Winsor, Jun'r., Uriah Arnold, Thomas Angel, Edward Manton, Jonathan Pike, Henry Randal, (son of Joseph,) Joseph Randal, (son of William,) James Clark, Thomas Olney, (son of Thomas,) John Ruttenburge, Joseph Nash, Joseph Whipple, Henry Eston, Nicholas Brown, Charles Smith, Gideon Brown, Jabez Gorham, Abel Peacy, David Tift, Joseph Kelton, Timothy Williams, Ebenezer Tyler, Charles Hickinbotham, John Owen, John Scott, Jun'r., Stephen Angel, Stukely Westcot, the third, William Hammond, Jeremiah Hawkins and Stephen Rawson.

### PORTSMOUTH.

Robert Burrington, Jun., and Joseph Cook.

### WARWICK.

Daniel Remington, Israel Arnold, (son of Elisha,) James Cook, Pentecost Sweet, Benjamin Sweet, Peleg Cook, Nathaniel Millard, Randal Holdon, Jun., Samuel Gorton, Thomas Tibbits, Amos Lockwood, Jun., Thomas Stone, William Wood and Anthony Holdon.

### WESTERLY.

Isaac Babcock, Robert Burdick, Jun., Joseph Witter, Jonathan Burdick, Joseph Burdick, Hubbard Burdick, (son of Robert,) Thomas Foster, Thomas Brand, Ezekiel Gavet, Jun., Edward Robinson, Benjamin Hall, Jonathan Palmittar, John West, John Maxson, Jun., John Cottril, William Hern, Jun., John Witter, Jun.,

Jedediah Davis, Nathan Lamphear, John Lamphear, Jun., Daniel Lamphear, William Clark, George Stillman, Jun., John Stillman, Elisha Stillman, Thomas Sisson, Jonathan Palmittar, Jun., Joseph Lewis, William Thompson, John Chapman, William Chapman, Jonathan Weaver, Jeremiah Crandel, Theodaty Vars, Cornelius Stutson, Roger White, Josias Hill, Jun., John Peckcom, John Pooler, John Hill, Christopher Edwards, Thomas Weaver, William Saunders, Jonathan Brown, Ebenezer Burdick and Samuel Maxson.

### NORTH KINGSTOWN.

Joseph Northup, Jun., John Briggs, Philip Tourjè and George Northup.

### SOUTH KINGSTOWN.

John Watson, Nathaniel Gardner, Jeremiah Wilcox, Jonathan Shearman, Moses Barber, Samuel Barber, Samuel Whaley, Peter Crandal, Stephen Cottril, Jun., Caleb Haszard, Ebenezer Brenton, John Rose, Joseph Haszard, Benjamin Perry, Jonathan Haszard, Thomas Haszard, (son of Jonathan, dec'ed.,) Jeremiah Haszard, and James Barber.

### EAST GREENWICH.

Benjamin Spenser, Jonathan Nichols, Jeremiah Spencer, William Davis, Samuel Sweet, Silas Jones, Jeremiah Spenser and Caleb Briggs.

### JAMESTOWN.

Gershom Remington, John Remington, (son of Gershom,) and Benjamin Carr, (son of Edward, deceas'd.)

### SMITHFIELD.

Joshua Smith, Joseph Latham, Ananias Mowrey, John Wilkinson, Jun., Isaac Medberry, Richard Aldrich and Noah Whitman.

### SCITUATE.

Peter Parker, Henry Randal, Samuel Smith, Charles Beers, John Young, Daniel Hopkins, Thomas Mathewson, William Young, Jonathan Angel, Jeremiah Brownel, Joseph Jenckes, John Randal, Joseph Knight, John Potter, Caleb Pearce, Benjamin Daley, Samuel Daley, Caleb Cory, Daniel Tift, David Brown, Elisha Barnes, Daniel Scott, Daniel Scott, Jun., Job Willbore and William Aldrich.

### GLOCESTER.

James King, Jun., David Thornton, Thomas King, Thomas Pollock, Samuel Short, John Benson, Benjamin Phetteplace, Elias Smith, Benjamin Mackintire, Titus Thornton, John Ross, Benjamin Warner, Nathaniel Kimbel, Valentine Inman, John Thornton, Noah Aldrich, Nehemiah Lewis, Ebenezer Cooke, William Colwell, Jeremiah Bellue and Joseph Eddy.

### CHARLESTOWN.

Benjamin Braman, Consider Halls, Stephen Johnson, Ezekiel Johnson, Robert Austin, Jun. and Job Taylor.

### WEST GREENWICH.

John Weaver, (son of William,) Anthony Goffe, Abner Goffe, Benjamin Sweet, Jun'r., John Case, (son of Joseph) and John Case, (son of John, son of Joseph.)

### COVENTRY.

Joseph Edmonds, Michael Stafford, Thomas Utter, Jonathan Green and Uriel Green, Jun'r.

### EXETER.

James Brayman, Solomon Brayman, Edward Greene and Jeoffrey Champlin, Jun'r.

### MIDDLETOWN.

John Greene, Jun'r., Joseph Ryder, Christopher Hawkins and James Phillips, Jun'r.

### BRISTOL.

Simon Davis, Jeremiah Wilson, Ephraim Tisdale, William Cox, Charles Munroe, Josiah Finney and Bosworth Kinnicut.

5

### TIVERTON.

John Manchester, Samuel Snell, Joseph Anthony, Roger Cory, Thomas Cook, Thomas Weight, Edward Wanton, John Borden, Samuel Durfie, Weston Hickes, Samuel Hickes, Stephen Cook, Thomas Howland, John Tabor, Cornelius Soule, Philip Cory, Thomas Cook, (son of Joseph,) George Cook, William Willcocks, John Almy, Ebenezer Tabor, John Bennet, Benjamin Durfie, Peter Talman, John Jennings, Abraham Barker, Samuel Borden, Restcome Sandford, Oliver Bailey, Samuel Snell, Jun'r., Joseph Tabor, John Tabor, (son of John,) Samuel Hart, Jonathan Hart, Joseph Wanton, John Cook, John Pearce, Peleg Shearman, Daniel Earl, David Durfie, Samuel Hart, Jun'r., Job Durfie, Joseph Stafford, David Stafford, Abraham Stafford, William Sandford, Peleg Sandford, Joshua Dwelly, Jun., Blake Perry, John Cook, (son of Thomas,) William Woodel, John Bowen, Samuel Shearman, William Shrieve, William Fish, William Manchester, (son of Stephen,) Joseph Crandal, Josiah Sawyer, David Lake, Joseph Jennings, Benjamin Maccomber, Phillip Tabor, Joseph Tabor, (son of Phillip,) Benjamin Chace, Jun'r., William Cook, Thomas Fish, William Corey, Jonathan Davel, George Westgate, Thomas Anthony, Caleb Cory, Thomas Grey, Phillip Gray, William Gray, John Brown, Thomas Wilcocks, Joshua Dwelly, Abner Chace, Josiah Wilcocks, Giles Brownel, William Springer, Gershom Woodel, Joseph Seabury, Samuel Almy, Thomas Crandal, Paul Tabor, Benjamin Hambly, Job Almy, William Manchester, (son of John,) Daniel Earl, Jun'r., John Sawyer, Oliver Cook, John Thomas, Ebenezer Shearman, Noah Davenport, Thomas Cook, (son of John Cook) and William Almy.

### LITTLE COMPTON.

Thomas Church, Israel Stoddard, Fobes Southworth, Robert Taylor, Jun'r., Joshua Hillard, Moses Palmer, David Hillard, Simeon Palmer, Job Brownel, Robert Brown, Jonathan Davenport, Abiel Cook, John Hart and Job Briggs.

### WARREN.

Bernard Miller, Benjamin Estabrook, Richard Hale, John Kinnicut, Jun'r., David Cole, Benjamin Cole and John Low.

## CUMBERLAND.

James Howard. Caleb Aldrich, Moses Arnold, Roger Hill, Jona-athan Jillson, Stephen Inman and Samuel Fisk.

## RICHMOND.

Stephen Wilcox, John Knowles, John Wilbore, Benjamin Potter, David Stanton. Joseph Kinyon, Ezekiel Tift, John Knowles, Jun'r., Nicholas Mosher, John Kinyon, (son of Joseph,) Thomas Mosher and Smiton Hart.

## 1774667

### APRIL 30, 1751.

Whereas all and every of the persons whose names hereafter follow, have taken the oath or affirmation prescribed by the colony law against bribery and corruption, in the choice of officers in the colony, it is therefore voted and resolved, That all and every of them be, and they are hereby admitted to give their votes to choose officers for their respective towns; and also to give their votes for the choice of the general officers of the government:—

## NEWPORT.

Peter Phillips, Benj. Chanders, Matthew Borden, Henry Freeborn, Augustus Johnston, William Thurston, Nathaniel Coggeshall, Jun'r., Joseph Tillinghast, (son of Jonathan,) Joseph Dunham and Preserved Fish.

## PROVIDENCE.

Benjamin Carpenter, George Potter, Peter Ranal, Caleb Potter, Benjamin Bowen. John Cumstock, Benjamin Man, Richard Coman, Henry Sweeting. Jun'r., John Fenner, Henry Sweeting, Timothy Sabin, Esek Hopkins, Richard Hoyle, Ambrose Page, Ezra Dean, David Brown, Joseph Allen, Jonathan Cumstock, Josiah Owen, Ezekiel Woodward. Ezekiel Woodward, Jun'r., James Field, John Thomas, Jun'r., Benjamin Catbeth, Stephen Sweet, Jun'r., Noah

Mason, John Waterman, the third, William Randal, Jun'r., Joseph
Sheldon, Jun'r., Isaac Olney, Nathan Jenckes, Timothy Sabin,
William Ashton, Jun'r., John Dunwell, James Angel, John Harris,
William Briggs, William Westcot, Jun'r., Nedebiah Angel, William
Clarke, Philip Potter, Thomas Westcot, Charles Rhoads, Samuel
Thurber, Charles Waterman, Peter Bateman, Jonathan Belue, Jo-
seph Rhoads, Daniel Matthewson, Joseph Potter, Stephen Smith,
Joseph Field, Jun'r., John Fenner, William Field, James Brown,
Anthony Olney, Peleg Arnold, John Wilkinson and James Mitchel,
Jun'r.

### PORTSMOUTH.

Noel Freeborn, John Borden and John Cook.

### WARWICK.

Joseph Philp, John Walton, Jun'r., Samuel Davis, Henry Tibbits, William Weaver, Daniel Scranton, William Edmonds and
James Green, (son of James.)

### WESTERLY.

William Crumb, Parsivel Allen, George Lanphear, Ebenezer
Hill, John Burdick, Matthew Maxson, Zacheus Pooler and William
Hadsel.

### NEW SHOREHAM

Simon Ray, Samuel Rathbun, Joseph Mitchel, Jun'r., Jonathan
Mitchel, Thomas Mitchel, Thomas Pain, John Pain, Thomas Dick-
ens, William Dodge, Samuel Dodge, Abel Franklin, Daniel Rose,
John Mott, Nathaniel Mott, Edward Sands, Robert Hull, Stephen
Franklin, Joshua Sands, Nathaniel Littlefield, Anthony Littlefield,
John Dodge, John Ball, Edward Ball, Samuel Dun, Caleb Little-
field, John Littlefield, Nathaniel Doge, Jun'r.

### NORTH KINGSTOWN.

John Slocum, Stephen Cooper, David Green, Robert Westgoat,
Jun'r., Jeremiah Fones, Christopher Phillips, Jun'r., John Cory,
Jun'r., John Cleveland, Joseph Northup, Jeremiah Haszard, Jun'r.,
Benoni Shearman, David Aldrich, Ezekiel Hunt, Jun'r., Samuel
Hunt, Jun'r., Richard Card, John Cole and Caleb Allen.

## SOUTH KINGSTOWN.

Samuel Rodman, Samuel Oatley, Daniel Tift, Job Reynolds, Samuel Curtis, Samuel Stedman, Thomas Potter and John Albro.

## EAST GREENWICH.

John Lion, Caleb Sheffield, Daniel Brown, Elijah Johnston, Thomas Langford, (son of John,) Edward Green, Joseph Matthewson, Benjamin Fry and James Runnels.

## JAMESTOWN.

Daniel Weeden, Jun'r., Josiah Arnold, Jun'r. and Benjamin Sheffield.

## SMITHFIELD.

Stephen Whipple, Abraham Smith, Seth Arnold, Edmund Arnold, Stephen Sayles, John Barnes, Nathaniel Herrenden, Robert Woodward, Daniel Wilbore, Jun'r., Henry Finch, Elisha Sayles, Edward Thayer, Daniel Cass, Nathan Cass, Joseph Cook, Jeremiah Cumstock, John Brown, Thomas Curff, Jun'r., Thomas Woodward, Joseph Buffum, Daniel Wilbore and Thomas Broadway.

## SCITUATE.

Stephen Sheldon, Zuriel Matthewson, Nicholas Hopkins, James Wheeler, David Yeau, Joseph Yeau, Daniel Bennet, Joseph Cole, Isaac King, Uriah Franklin, Nathaniel Hareden, William Blanchard, Jun'r., Bernard Hale, Francis Fuller, Joseph Waterman, Adam Casey, Edward Casey, Nathan Bennet and James Round.

## GLOCESTER.

Samuel Sprague, Joshua King, Benjamin King, Ezra Thornton, Samuel Irons, John Davis, John Aldrich, Daniel Whipple, Samuel Short, Jun'r., Eleazer Crassman, Ebenezer Jencks, Israel Sayles, Nathan Wade and Ezekiel Sayles.

## WEST GREENWICH.

Henry Straight, John Niles and John Dolliver.

### COVENTRY.

. Ichabod Bowen, Thomas Eddy, James Green, (son of Daniel,) Josiah Gibbs and Joseph Bennet.

### EXETER.

Samuel Sweet, Caleb Gardner and Robert Moon, Jun'r.

### MIDDLETOWN.

Peter Barker, Peter Barker, Jun'r., Henry Tew and William Bliss.

### BRISTOL.

George Coggeshall, John Waldron, John Chaloner and John In-graham.

### TIVERTON.

Timothy Clossen, John Dennis, Gideon Willcock, Joseph Tabor, (tanner,) George Westgate, Jun'r., Robert Burrington, Joseph Cook, Charles Brownel, Isaac Barker and Stephen Talman.

### WARREN.

John Braley, William Hill, Isaac Cole, Nathan Cole, Stephen Bowen and Simeon Peck.

### CUMBERLAND.

Ibrook Whipple, Nathaniel Robinson, Enoch Whetherhead, Ab-ner Ballou, Joseph Darling, Richard Peters and Thomas Hill.

### RICHMOND.

Stephen Sweet, William Watson, Joseph Hoxsie, Jun'r., John Thomas and Nathaniel Pettis.

N. B.—Charlestown and Little Compton, made no returns this election.

## MAY 5th, 1752.

Whereas, the persons whose names hereafter follow, have taken the oath or affirmation prescribed by the colony law against bribery and corruption, it is therefore voted and resolved, That all and every of them be, and they are hereby admitted free and enabled to give their votes to choose officers in their respective towns, and also to give their votes for the choice of general officers of the government:—

### NEWPORT.

Francis Pope, Benjamin Almy, John Tripp, John Vial, Lemuel Wyatt, John Collins, Ebenezer Vorce, Peleg Chapman, Thomas Weeden, Benjamin Day, Lawrence Clark, Jun'r., Peter James, Joshua Amy, Joseph Wilson, Griffin Barney, John Phillips, John Greene, Charles Bowler, Thomas Richardson, (son of Ebenezer,) Jonas Langford Redwood, Metcalf Bowler and John Reed, (son of William.)

### PROVIDENCE.

James Swane, James Fenner, John Hopkins, Jeremiah Hawkins, William Compton, Theophilus Williams, John Thomas, Stephen Wright, Robert Gibbs, Jun'r., Benjamin Smith, Abraham Belknap, Nathaniel Sweeting, Thomas Waterman, Robert Young, Gilbert Simmons, William Edmonds, Thomas Kilton, Obediah Brown, (the third,) William Page, Jun'r., Stephen Kilton, Samuel Fish, Samuel Nightingale, Josiah King, Nathaniel Waterman, Jun'r., Richard Knight, (the fourth,) Nathaniel Packard, John Briggs, Archibar Wear, Timothy Miles, William Kilton, Richard Olney, Eleazer Greene, Ezra Olney, Jeremiah Burlingame, Benoni Pearce, Samuel Westcot, (son of Jabez,) John Williams, (son of Thomas,) Guias Davis, Peleg Rhodes, John Anthony Angell, Samuel Burlingame, John Manton, Jun'r., Jesse Beverly, Gideon Olney and Nathaniel Jacobs.

### PORTSMOUTH.

John Lawton.

### WARWICK.

John Ladd, Joshua Greene, John Waterman and David Chace.

### WESTERLY.

Samuel Brand and Ebenezer Lamb.

### NEW SHOREHAM.

Edmund Sheffield, Ezekiel Sheffield, William Dodge, Jun'r. and Tormat Rose.

### NORTH KINGSTOWN.

Samuel Spink, David Greene, Jun'r., James Hyams, Ebenezer Briggs, Joshua Pearce, Edward Dyre, (son of Edward Dyre, Jun'r.,) Josiah Godfrey, William Thomas, Benjamin Congdon, (son of Benjamin Congdon, Jun'r.,) David Vaughan, Israel Phillips, Eber Shearman, Jun'r., John Reynolds, (son of James,) Isaac Vaughan, Stephen Herrington, Ezekiel Hunt, Samuel Hunt and William Shearman.

### SOUTH KINGSTOWN.

William Case, Benjamin Watson, Daniel Stedman, Nathaniel Mumford, George Haszard, Job Babcock, (son of Samuel,) Jeremiah Wilson, Job Babcock, (the third,) Timothy Lock, David Babcock, (the third,) William Robinson, James Perry, Jun'r., Robert Knowles, Jun'r., Richard Haszard and Samuel Casey.

### EAST GREENWICH.

Daniel Brown, Robert Nichols and Silas Jones.

### SMITHFIELD.

Robert Woodward, Daniel Wilbore, Jun'r., Henry Finch, Elisha Sayles, John Brown, Daniel Cass, Nathan Cass, Joseph Cook, Jeremiah Comstock, Thomas Cruff, Jun'r., Thomas Woodward, Joseph Buffum, Daniel Wilbore, Thomas Broadway, Andrew Waterman, Joshua Phillips, Jeremiah Phillips, John Whiteman, Gideon Dexter, Winchester Matthewson, Samuel Goldthwait, James Mussey, Benjamin Ballard, Nathan Cass, James Leonard. Ephraim Whipple, Robert Woodward, Joshua Arnold and John Ballou, Jun'r.

## GLOCESTER.

Joshua Eddy, Obediah Jencks, Jonathan Eddy, Peleg Chace, William Havens, Jeremiah Steere, Benjamin Keach, Jun'r., Ezra Bartlet, Jun'r., John Steere, Jun'r., Jonah Steere, John Steere, Jonathan Tourtelot, Job Armstrong, Oliver Winslow, Stephen Keach. Benjamin Tourtelot, Joseph Sprague, Nathan Pain, Thomas Herenden, Joseph Colvell, Israel Thornton, Timothy Sweet, Obediah Bowen, Joshua Salisbury, Jerem'h. Irons, Silas Williams, Abraham Clark, Chad Brown, Enoch Whipple, Joseph Cowen, Noah Arnold, Edward Inman, Jun'r., Samuel Ross and William Ross.

## CHARLESTOWN.

Robert Potter, Gideon Hoxsie and John Holloway.

## WEST GREENWICH.

Abraham Laja, Peter Lee, Robert Hopkins, James Hopkins, Jonathan Weaver, Benjamin Greene, (son of Henry,) John Matthewson, (son of Henry Matthewson, Jun'r.,) Ephraim Hayward. Job Kerrington, Jonathan Aylsworth, and Benjamin Greene.

## COVENTRY.

Joseph Bennet, Jun'r., Silas Wood, Daniel Walker, Nicholas Ide, Joab Stafford, Valentine Mors, Robert Love, Benjamin Vaughan and Charles Andrew, (son of Charles.)

## EXETER.

Jeremiah Rogers, Edward Wilcox, William Barber. Jonathan Babcock, Jeremiah Austin, (the third,) Thomas Gardner, Jun'r., John Potter, Jun'r. and Jeremiah Allen.

## MIDDLETOWN.

Handley Chipman.

6

### LITTLE COMPTON.

Thomas Brownel, Jun'r., Giles Pearce, John Simmons, Noah Stoddard, Isaac Simmonds, Jonathan Records, Ephraim Richmond, William Richmond, Jun'r., Perez Richmond, Stephen Brownel, Pearce Brownel, Israel Shaw, Thomas Dring, Constant Church and James Bennet.

### CUMBERLAND.

Jeremiah Arnold, Jonathan Aldrich, Christopher Bullock and Daniel Smith, Jun'r.

### RICHMOND.

George Lewis, Elisha Babcock and Thomas Kinyon, Jun'r.

## MAY 1st, 1753.

Whereas all and every of the persons whose names hereafter follow, have taken the oath or affirmation prescribed by the colony law against bribery and corruption in the choice of officers in this colony, it is therefore voted and resolved that all and every of them be and they are hereby admitted to give their votes to choose officers for their respective towns, and also to give their votes in the choice of the general officers of the government:—

### NEWPORT.

Peleg Clarke, John Warren, (son of Joseph,) William Allen, the carver, Abraham Brownel, George Burkmaster, Joseph Wanton, Jun'r., (son of Joseph,) Thomas Cornel, James Linscomb and John Hicks.

### PROVIDENCE.

John Jenckes, Jun'r., Christopher Hopkins, Joseph Dexter, John Lawrence, Grindal Rawson, Isaac Corey, Joseph Lawrance, Ezra Hutchins, Alexander Frazier, Jun'r., Ephraim Wheaton, Jeremiah

Brown, Noah Whipple, Benjamin Brown, John Hartshorn, Ephraim Carpenter, John Sheldon, Thomas Simmons, Nehemiah Allen, Elisha Greene, Jun'r., Joseph Sweeting, John Sweet, John Scott, Samuel Angel, Zachariah Eddy, Abraham Smith, Job Hawkins, James Thurber, Anthony Field, Levi Simmons, John King, Thomas Manchester, Jun'r., Josiah Westcot, Elijah Bacon, George Beverly, Joseph Thornton, Jun'r., David Burr, Joseph Carpenter, Ephraim Congdon, Job Sheldon, Israel Gorton, Jun'r., Robert Magill, Stephen Jackson, George Jackson, Daniel Snow, James Snow, Eziekel Williams, Giles Peckham, Isaac Belknap, Cornelius Easton, Jun'r. and Peter Stone.

### PORTSMOUTH.

Giles Cook and Peleg Sisson.

### WARWICK.

Amos Warner, Joseph Greene, John Lippit, Solomon Howard, Peleg Rice, James Converse, James Arnold, (son of Elisha,) and Thomas Tibbitts.

### WESTERLY.

William Smith, William Pendleton, Jun'r., Joseph Greene, Edward Bliven, Jun'r., Elisha Clark, Jonathan Wells, John Robinson, Thomas Brand, Jun'r., Samuel Champlin, Joseph Clarke, Jun'r., William Hiscox, Jun'r., John Burdick and Peter Kinyon.

### SOUTH KINGSTOWN.

John Records, Christopher Robinson, George Willson, Oliver Helme, Samuel Seagers, Job Card, Francis Tanner, Matthew Robinson, John Crandal, Isaac Sheldon, Job Card, Jun'r., John Douglas, Jonathan Shearman, Jun'r. and Samuel Hopkins.

### EAST GREENWICH.

Samuel Tarbor, Fones Whitford, Preserved Pearce, Jun'r., Robert Baley, Francis Barker, Nathaniel Briggs, John Roberts, John Nichols, Robert Vaughan, John Tarbox.

### SMITHFIELD.

Stephen Arnold, Jun'r., Daniel Aldrich, Joseph Kelly, Benjamin Medberry, Richard Sayles, Hezekiah Sprague, Jacob Smith, Francis Herrenden, Philip Loja, John Cumstock, Daniel Mowry, Jun'r., Simeon Brown, David Arnold, Jonathan Sayles and David Smith.

### SCITUATE.

John Colvin, Nathaniel Wells, Ezekiel Westcot and Levi Preston.

### GLOCESTER.

Jonathan Harris, Rufus Smith, Ephraim Pierce and Ebenezer Darling.

### CHARLESTOWN.

Samuel Burdick, Salter Putman, Samuel Burdick, Jun'r., Amos Lewis, John Stanton and Joseph Willcox.

### WEST GREENWICH.

James Briggs and Job Herrington.

### COVENTRY.

Matthew Patrick, Willson Key, Aaron Bowen, Jun'r., Thomas Whaley, Samuel Greene, Thomas Waterman, Josias Streeter, Timothy Green and John Greene, (son of Ebenezer.)

### EXETER.

Jonathan Lewis and Stephen Albro.

### MIDDLETOWN.

William Turner, Jun'r., Thomas Gould, Jun'r., Thomas Coggeshall, Jun'r. and William Baily.

### BRISTOL.

Leveret Hubbard, Samuel Church, Joseph Eddy, Daniel Waldron, Jonathan Munday, William Emmerson and Aaron Bourn.

## LITTLE COMPTON.

Ichabod Stodard, Eliphalet Davenport, John Bennet, George Wood, John Wood, Jun'r. and Nathaniel Pearce.

## TIVERTON.

Lovet Briggs and Thomas Tabor.

## WARREN.

William Cole, Nathaniel Peck, Jun'r., Nathaniel Toogood and John Davis.

## CUMBERLAND.

James Tilson, Andrew Dexter, Ichabod Scott, Jeremiah Scott, Elisha Ballou, Benjamin Farrington and Jonathan Gaskill.

## RICHMOND.

David Larkin, Thomas Potter, Jun'r. and John Thomas.

## APRIL 30th, 1754.

Whereas, all and every of the persons whose names hereafter follow, have (taken) the oath or affirmation prescribed by the colony law against bribery and corruption, in the choice of officers in this colony, it is therefore voted and resolved, that all and every of them be and they are hereby admitted to give their votes to choose officers for their respective towns, and also to give their votes in the choice of the general officers of the government :—

## NEWPORT.

Ezra Pope, Thomas Ayres, Clement Peckom, David M'quellem, Silas Cook, Francis Honyman, Robert Crooke, Benjamin Wickham, Joseph Brown, Benjamin Thurston, Timothy Ingraham, Matthew Borden, (son of Abraham,) Thomas Rodman, (son of Clark,) Benjamin Atwood, John Lyon, Jun., Valentine Thurston, John

Allison, Isaac Stelle, Joshua Saunders, Barzilla Bailey, Thomas
Melvill, Jun., Thomas George, Anthony Shaw, Jonathan Clarke,
(goldsmith,) Benjamin Jefferson, John Cook, Israel Woodward,
Samuel Greene, Peter Phillips, (merchant,) Joseph Cozzens, Con-
stant Cook, Ebenezer Trobridge, Jahleel Brenton, Jun., William
Paul, Daniel Whitman Hoockey, Lewis Ginedo, Joshua Hacker,
Thomas Moffatt, John Grelea, Jun., Nathan Chapman, William
Allen, Eleazer Read, John Tayre, (son of Benjamin,) Benjamin
Ingraham, George Gardner,. (son of John,) William Cranston,
William Thurston Gardner, Elisha Sanford, Jun., Nathaniel Tay-
lor, Israel Casswell, Joseph Boss, Samuel Hull, Jun., Nathaniel
Mumford, Peter Treby, Timothy Witherly, John M'Daniel, Samuel .
Rhodes, Benjamin Brown, James Pitman, Samuel Rhodes, (mason,)
William Pelsue. Joseph Gladding, Jun. and John James, Jun., (son
of John, Cordwainer.)

## PROVIDENCE.

William Jencks, Thomas Whipple, Eliphalet Philbrook, Mosses
Smith, Elisha Arnold, John Randall, Jeremiah Brown, Peter Cook,
Samuel Relph, Benjamin Sprague, Jun., Maturin Bellau, John
Jencks, Nathaniel Waterman, Edward Sarles, Alexander Maccarey,
Elisha Hale, Ichabod Jencks, James Briggs, Jun., Joseph Manches-
ter, Josiah Westcot, Jun., Joseph Lockwood, Daniel Abbot, Jun.,
John Smith, John Kinnicut, Solomon Searle, Consider Luther, Mar-
tin Salsbury, Nehemiah Smith, Ephraim Whipple, Daniel Smith,
Jun., Edward Smith, Jabez Pierce, Daniel Whipple, Stephen
Wright, William Donnison, Jeremiah Westcot, (cooper.) David
Burr, Josiah Burlinggame, James Seamons, John Seamons, Simon
Read, Samuel Read, John Lovet, Nathan Olney, Thomas Perry,
Amos Hopkins, Jun., John Ormes, Ephraim Congdon, Thomas
Field, Jun., Joshua Burlinggame, Joseph Smith, George Curlis,
Simon Smith, Samuel Jackson, John Power, Thomas Williams,
John Cole, Amos Hopkins, John Smith and Jonathan Mowrey.

## PORTSMOUTH.

John Brightman, George Cornel, (son of Walter,) John Earl, -
George Brownwell, Restcom Sanford and Joseph Cundall, Jun'r.

## WARWICK.

Sion Arnold, John Low, (son of Stephen,) Peter Worden, Caleb Gorton, Thomas Arnold, Nathaniel Hillard, Eleazer Chace, Stephen Arnold, Benjamin Greene, (son of John,) David Knap, William Godfrey, Samuel Finney, Samuel Gorton, (son of Samuel) and John Stafford.

## WESTERLY.

Joshua Lanphear, Ezekiel Hall, Christopher Wilbore, William Maxson, Daniel Butler, Nathan McCoon, Samuel Larkin, Joseph Hiscox, Samuel Button, Jun. and Timothy Porter.

## NORTH KINGSTOWN.

Alexander Brown, Jun., Jonathan Card, Joshua Allen, Ebenezer Smith, Thomas Eldred (son of William,) Thomas Smith, John Huling, Charles Tillinghast, Carey Clarke, Jun., George Vaughan, Benjamin Congdon, (son of Joseph,) Elnathan Sweet, Silvester Havens, Silvester Hyams, Matthew Cooper and Matthew Allen.

## SOUTH KINGSTOWN.

Thomas Rodman, Joseph Knowles, Benjamin Rodman, Benjamin Weight, Joseph Seager, Edward Perrey, Gideon Casey, Jeremiah Crandall, John Hazzard, Charles Hull, George Babcock, Jun., James Gardner, Peter Boss, Jun., Benjamin Boss, William Wilcox, Benjamin Shearman and Freeman Perry.

## EAST GREENWICH.

Joshua Rathbun, David Sweet, George Weaver, William Bently, Joseph Carpenter, Josiah Burlingame, Jun., Joseph Carpenter, John Aylsworth, Joseph Corey, Thomas Spencer, (son of Benjamin,) William Bently, George Weaver, Nicholas Spencer, Thomas Place, Thomas Place, Jun., Thomas Briggs and George Wightman.

## JAMESTOWN.

Thomas Bently, Isaac Howland and David Greene.

## SMITHFIELD.

Caleb Smith, Reuben Aldrich, Samuel Cruff, Edmund Jenckes, Peter Tifft, Joseph Cumstock, Jonathan Sprague, Hazadiah Cumstock, Jeremiah Arnold, Amos Sprague, Joseph Herrenden, Daniel Smith, (son of Elisha,) Abraham Scott, Maturin Ballow, John Phillips, Peter Tifft, Caleb Smith, Jonathan Read, Samuel Cruff, Nathan Tucker, Joseph Comstock, Benjamin Buffum, Edmund Jenckes, Benjamin Burton, Benjamin Slocum, Abiah Angel, Jacob Arnold, Joshua Lapham, Hazadiah Cumstock, Jun., Richard Plumer, Enoch Sprague, Robert Woodward, William Staples and Daniel Arnold.

## SCITUATE.

Robert Potter, Hugh Relph, Nathan Young, Jeremarth Hopkins, Isaac Howard, Stephen Foster, Joseph Herrenden, Jun., Enoch Place, Nathan Place, Hugh Pray, Stephen Williams, Benjamin Wight, the third, Thomas Collins, (son of Eleazer,) Joseph Berry, Thomas Hill, Jonathan Knight, James Matthewson, Robert Potter, Jun., Jabez Relph, Richard Pray, Amos Herrendon, Benjamin Vaughan, Robert Williams and Esquire Bucklin.

## GLOCESTER.

John Wells, Jeremiah Phillips, Jun., Joseph Aldrich, Obadiah Lewis, Jeremiah Sweet, Hezekiah Tinckom, Joseph Richardson, Goliath Williams, Eliphalet Eddy, Samuel Phetteplace, Reuben Coombes, Ebenezer Sailsbury, John Johnson, Joseph Albec, Jeremiah Cumstock, Richard Smith, Jun., Joseph Smith, Enoch Smith, Nehemiah Bellue, Peter Bellue, Nathaniel Man, Robert Saunders, Solomon Smith, John Hunt, Elkanath Shearman, Peter Place and Benjamin Thornton, Jun.

## CHARLESTOWN.

Edward Perry, John Perry, James Congdon, the third, Joseph Champlin, John Millard, Jun., William Harvey, John Adams and John Adams, Jun.